THE LOCKED ROOM

HOLLY HEPBURN

B
Boldwood

First published in Great Britain in 2026 by Boldwood Books Ltd.

Cover Design by Lizzie Gardiner

Cover Images: Shutterstock and Adobe Stock

A CIP catalogue record for this book is available from the British Library.

Paperback ISBN 978-1-83533-763-9

Large Print ISBN 978-1-83533-764-6

Hardback ISBN 978-1-83533-762-2

Trade Paperback ISBN 978-1-80656-272-5

Ebook ISBN 978-1-83533-765-3

Kindle ISBN 978-1-83533-766-0

Audio CD ISBN 978-1-83533-757-8

MP3 CD ISBN 978-1-83533-758-5

Digital audio download ISBN 978-1-83533-759-2

This book is printed on certified sustainable paper. Boldwood Books is dedicated to putting sustainability at the heart of our business. For more information please visit https://www.boldwoodbooks.com/about-us/sustainability/

Boldwood Books Ltd, 23 Bowerdean Street, London, SW6 3TN
www.boldwoodbooks.com

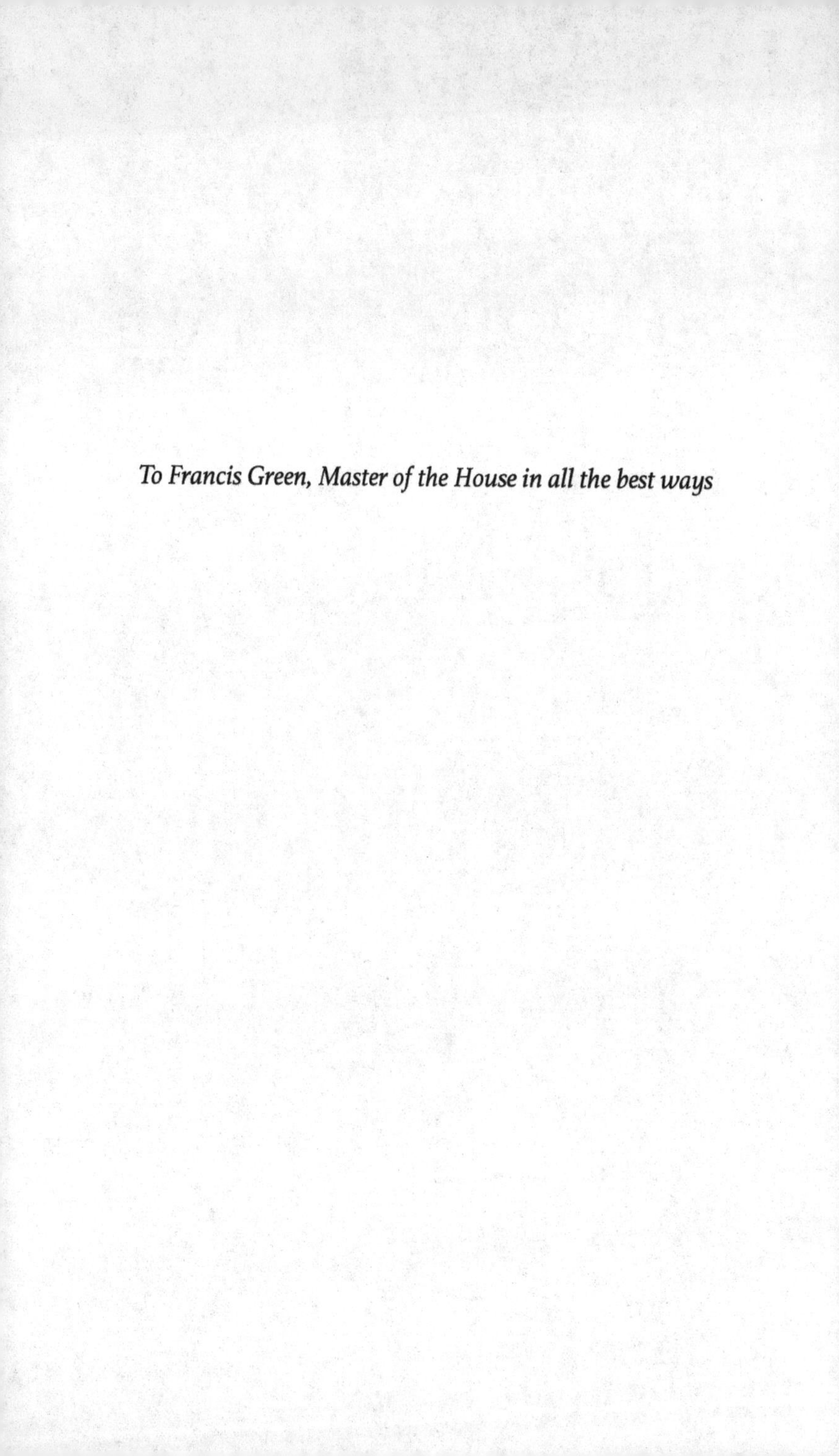

To Francis Green, Master of the House in all the best ways

AUTHOR'S NOTE

If you've read the other *Baker Street Mysteries*, you'll know that the premise of these stories is based on a real-life scenario. In 1932, the Abbey Road Building Society moved into their new headquarters in the heart of London. The offices spanned numbers 219 to 229 Baker Street, which any fan of crime fiction knows includes a very famous address, and sure enough, the bank immediately began to receive letters addressed to Mr Sherlock Holmes. There were so many that they were forced to employ someone to reply – a secretary to Holmes who played along with the belief that the great detective was a real person – and the role continued for many decades, perhaps even until the bank left Baker Street in 2002. The *Baker Street Mysteries* imagines a secretary tempted to investigate some of the letters on Sherlock's behalf, with hopefully entertaining results.

I'm afraid I've taken the tiniest of creative liberties with Gordon's Wine Bar, which regrettably does not have velvet-curtained nooks for clandestine encounters, and with the Theatre Royal, Drury Lane, which may not have a subterranean costume store. The cellars of Quaglino's, on the other hand, do exist and they were used for decades to lay down bottles of wine for regular customers, just as Harry and Oliver observe. A little bird tells me that these cellars were part of a network of tunnels beneath Mayfair – legend has it they extended all the way to St James's Palace. Naturally, I couldn't wait to incorporate this titbit into a story, but the descriptions in this book are entirely products of my imagination.

Lastly, the lurid history of 50 Berkeley Square is well worth a few minutes of your time, should you have access to the internet and an interest in the macabre. Let's just say Welcome Dobbs was not wrong when he warned Harry to steer clear...

Holly Hepburn
January 2026

'It is stupidity rather than courage to refuse to recognise danger when it is close upon you.'

— ARTHUR CONAN DOYLE, *THE FINAL PROBLEM*

1

There were several occurrences during Harry White's tenure as Secretary to Sherlock Holmes that she looked back on with sadness and regret, but perhaps none quite so much as the dark and twisted events that unfolded in Mayfair at the start of January 1933. As ever, the matter began with a letter addressed to the great detective. What differed was that this letter was not delivered to the Abbey Road Building Society, whose head offices incorporated number 221b Baker Street, London. Instead, it was printed among the agony columns of *The Times* newspaper on New Year's Day, and it did not beg for help. In evident homage to the works of the late Sir Arthur Conan Doyle, it threw down an intriguing gauntlet.

> My dear Sherlock Holmes,
>
> You are invited to prove your status as the world's greatest detective by solving an impossible crime. You have seven days.
>
> Yours sincerely,
>
> Professor James Moriarty

Harry had to concede it was nicely done as she studied the appeal by the soft glow of the table lamps in the library of her family home. In the world of Holmes and Watson, the personal columns of the daily newspapers were a frequent fascination to the great detective; had this been the start of one of their adventures, Harry had no doubt the pair would be roused to immediate action by such a challenge from their arch-nemesis, the shadowy Moriarty. But in reality, there was no such person as Sherlock Holmes, nor a Professor Moriarty, leading Harry to surmise the letter was a prank, or a private game amongst friends, as many messages placed in the agony columns were. It certainly could not be intended for her. Admittedly, she had been tempted to investigate one or two cases that had stood out from the vast correspondence Holmes received at the bank each day, but she had done so secretly, maintaining the pretence that the detective was real, and using an assumed name. It had been a terrible risk to deviate from the standard response she was supposed to send – discovery would cost both her job and the small independence she had carved out from her loving, if traditionally minded family – but the thrill of cracking each case had been worth it. Only a handful of people had met R. K. Moss, dauntless assistant to the now elderly Sherlock Holmes, and they were sworn never to reveal who had resolved their difficulties, or how it had been done. No, Harry thought as she studied Moriarty's message again, it was not aimed at her. How could it be?

'Good lord, you're not still taking in the news, are you?' Harry looked up to see her brother Sebastian framed in the doorway, arched eyebrows underscoring his amusement as he regarded her. 'I had no idea the deplorable state of the world gripped you so feverishly. Or is the crossword giving you trouble?'

Harry hid a smile. She'd had to wait for her father, her uncle and her eldest brother, Lawrence, to finish with the newspaper before she had been able to surreptitiously squirrel it away in the library, and they had all read it from the front page to the last. Her father would be Baron Abinger one day and Lawrence would eventually inherit the title from him; both took the responsibility seriously and kept abreast of the news. Seb, on the other hand, embraced his status as a second son with the happy understanding that responsibility was something for other people to worry about. He was not wild or wayward, like their youngest brother, Rufus, who was constantly teetering on the brink of scandal or disaster, but he was very rarely serious about anything. Seb's preferred reading matter was the society pages and gossip columns of less salubrious publications than the lofty *Times* and he was perfectly content to admit it. 'Three across,' Harry said, gazing down thoughtfully as though the page before her did indeed contain the fabled cryptic crossword. 'Sounds like the best day of the week to drink. Seven letters, starts with a T.'

Seb laughed. 'Very clever. And you're sort of in luck. Mama sent me to find you – she's organising charades in the drawing room. Thirsty or not, we'll all need a stiff drink to get through that.'

Harry groaned. Their mother was relentlessly sociable and loved nothing better than playing hostess to the many guests she invited to Abinger Hall. Thankfully, it had been a select group for New Year's Eve and most of them had shown the good manners to depart immediately after lunch, even if they had looked slightly the worse for wear. 'Are the Honeywells still here?' she asked Seb.

'Not so lucky there, I'm afraid. Mama hasn't given up hope of you and Philip hitting it off, although I don't think she's really thought it through. His mother would love to claim a close familial connection to the Abinger name.' He shuddered. 'Can you imagine? She'd cling on like a limpet.'

It was possibly a little unkind, Harry thought, but she couldn't deny he had a point. Eugenia Honeywell had a reputation as a social climber, intent on being associated with all the best families, and she made no secret of her desire to orchestrate a wedding between Harry and her son. But while Harry had nothing against Philip, who was generally inoffensive if occasionally patronising, she had no intention of marrying him or anyone else. At least not yet. She liked her job, she loved her little apartment in Mayfair and she cherished her freedom – all things she would have to give up if she married. And there was the small matter of not having met the right man. Her mother wouldn't begrudge Harry marrying for love, as long as the man she fell in love with had prospects and came from the right sort of family. 'I don't think Mama is serious about Philip. She wants to stir up the competition, that's all.'

Seb winked. 'Those charming Finchem boys, you mean? I'm not sure she needs to do much stirring there – I saw the way they looked at you the last time they were here. Like a pair of wolves who'd happened upon a defenceless lamb.'

The description irked Harry. All three of her brothers seemed to be of the wearying opinion that she needed protection, despite the fact that she had most certainly given as good as she'd got when they were growing up. What would they say if they'd seen her dashing through the murky, frozen waters of Morden Fen to launch herself at a would-be murderer? How would they react if they knew she had pursued a violent criminal through the grimy back streets of Elephant and Castle, with no thought for her own safety? Lawrence would be horrified, Seb would take her to task over the unfashionable clothing she'd worn, and Rufus would probably ask to join her. But she could never confide in any of them; her exploits as R. K. Moss had to remain a secret. The only person who knew the truth was Oliver Fortescue, successful city lawyer and her reluctant accomplice in the two cases she had investigated so far. He'd underestimated her abilities at first but she hoped he had more respect for her now. He'd stopped telling her off, at least. Mostly.

Even so, Harry knew what Seb meant about Percy and James Finchem. Separated in age by a few years, they were devilishly good looking, with dark hair, strong jawlines and an easy charm that she suspected hid a ruthless determination to get what they wanted. Percy used humour to his advantage, while James relied on gentlemanly admiration and flattery, which led his brother to accuse him of fancying himself a Mr Darcy. They had both demonstrated an admirable ability to flirt, vying for Harry's attention with an intensity that made her head spin, but Percy had seemed the more daring and she had to admit she'd enjoyed the attention. She had no intention of revealing that to Seb, however. 'I can handle them.'

'I have no doubt,' he said mildly. 'You play chess with Grandfather, which means you can run rings round the rest of us mere mortals.'

She smiled. Chess matches with their grandfather had been known to last for weeks and continue by letter when she was back in London, each detailing their move using the widely recognised chess notation system. Unfortunately, she rarely won. 'I'm not sure chess helps much in matters of the heart.'

His eyes narrowed slightly. 'No, I suppose not. Which reminds me, you haven't asked to borrow my car for ages. Did things peter out with your man in the village?'

Trying not to blush, Harry did her best to look like the kind of woman who might indulge in a passionate affair with the local blacksmith. She could hardly correct his bawdy assumption and admit the truth, which was that she had borrowed the MG to track down clues in the case of the missing maid. 'Oh. Well, it came to a natural conclusion,' she said, as airily as she could manage. 'No hard feelings on either side.'

'Good for you,' he said, grinning. 'But I won't pry any more. Everyone deserves to have secrets, even my little sister.' His smile dimmed. 'And speaking of secrets, there is something unfortunate we need to address once we're back in London.'

Instantly, Harry's scalp prickled. He couldn't suspect what she'd really been up to. He couldn't. 'Oh? What is it?'

But Seb shook his head. 'Not here. We'll have dinner one evening when we can talk properly.' He eyed her with undisguised regret. 'Some hard choices may need to be made, for the good of everyone.'

Heart thudding, Harry raised her chin in defiance. 'You can't make me choose anything.'

'Who said anything about you?' he said, blinking in astonishment. 'I'm talking about Rufus, you goose. It seems he's got himself tangled up with a gold digger.'

* * *

The Surrey fields were white with frost on Monday morning as Harry made her way back to London. The train was busy, filled with commuters returning to work after the New Year celebrations and Harry thought herself lucky to have bagged a seat beside the window, through which she watched the countryside whizz past. And whizz it did – the electrification of the line some three years earlier had made the journey considerably faster, although Harry found she missed the comforting chug-

chug-chug of the steam locomotive. Often, the rumble of the engine had served to soothe away the edges of a chaotic visit at Abinger Hall. It wasn't that she didn't enjoy being with her family, more that the occasional clash of headstrong personalities could produce sparks that ignited otherwise dormant tensions. On Sunday evening, she had overheard a ferocious argument between her mother and Rufus that she guessed must be to do with the bombshell Seb had dropped, and the resulting iciness between them had created a tension that had almost soured the wine at dinner. Harry had tried to lighten the mood by asking Rufus about his trip to Scotland but he had remained monosyllabic and simmering, and eventually she had given up. All of which meant she was more than a little relieved to be returning to London, where no one glowered at her if she asked them to pass the salt.

As the minutes ticked by, Harry turned her attention to her fellow passengers. All were unremarkable at first glance but she amused herself by studying them over the top of the book she was pretending to read, trying to elicit their secrets as Holmes or sharp-eyed Miss Marple would. The man sitting directly opposite was someone important in the City, Harry felt; his black bowler hat, wooden-handled umbrella and neatly folded overcoat were obviously the uniform of a gentleman banker. A leather briefcase rested beside his highly polished shoes. When he turned the page of the newspaper he was reading, she caught a glimpse of weighty jowls and florid cheeks on either side of a slightly crooked nose that suggested it had been broken at some time in the past. Perhaps he'd been a boxer in his youth. He might even enjoy gambling on such matches now.

Her gaze moved on to the next passenger, a young woman in a plain blue day dress and a cloche hat. She too had a coat across her lap and a pair of sensible shoes on her feet. Her brown hair was neatly curled beneath the hat and her face was expertly powdered and rouged. Imitation pearl earrings matched the string she wore around her neck. A Selfridges shop assistant, Harry decided, although she might just as easily be a secretary or even a nanny. Holmes was always so accurate in his observations of the people he encountered while solving his mysteries, plucking truths seemingly from thin air and astonishing all around him. But, as Harry had observed on many occasions in the months since she'd begun to tackle the mountain of letters that had amassed in the Abbey Road Building Society post room, it was easy to be brilliant when you were written that way.

At length, the train pulled into Waterloo station, depositing its tide of passengers onto the platform to disperse throughout the city. Harry took the Underground to Baker Street and made her way to the towering white façade of the bank. Opening in 1932, no expense had been spared in the construction of the building society's flagship offices; from the tall, intricately carved lighthouse statue inlaid above the grand entrance to the marbled lobby and gilded lift that served the upper floors, every effort had been made to assure potential investors that their money would be in very safe hands. Beyond the public areas, Harry had always enjoyed the ordered predictability of her work. It had never stretched her, not even when she had occupied the coveted position of personal assistant to Mr Simeon Pemberton, but she had enjoyed knowing that every task had been completed in a timely and highly professional way. It was a shame Mr Pemberton had turned out to be significantly less professional. The ensuing connection between her knee and his ardour had seen her demoted to the post room, located in the basement, and it was only through the kindness of her new manager, Mr Babbage, that she was not there still. Declaring immediately that the post room was no place for a young woman, he had found Harry a tiny, forgotten office on the second floor and arranged for Holmes' letters to be delivered to her there. It was a compromise Harry was still grateful for. Her new office was quiet, ignored by everyone except Bobby the post boy, and it was hers alone.

'Good morning, Miss White,' Patrick the doorman said cheerfully as she passed by. 'Happy New Year.'

'And to you,' Harry said. 'Did you have an enjoyable Christmas?'

Patrick nodded. 'I did, thank you. Took the family to the circus over East London and had an elegant time.'

'I'm delighted to hear it,' Harry replied warmly.

She glanced towards the other doorman, Danny, but he kept his chin tucked inside the black woollen scarf that swathed his neck and lower face as he mumbled an unintelligible greeting. Harry supposed she could hardly blame him; it was thanks to her that his face and hands were stained purple with gentian violet, although he'd brought it on himself by breaking into her office several weeks earlier and triggering the trap she had laid. The dye would eventually fade, she'd reassured him when he'd confronted her after the crime. She imagined his shame would take longer to disappear.

At the door to her office, Harry paused the way she now did every morning to assess the rudimentary burglar alarm she set upon leaving. The golden hair caught between the door and its frame was still in place. Satisfied, she fitted the key into the lock and entered. If Danny's intrusion had taught her anything, it was that she could not be too cautious in hiding her efforts at detective work. Both the Longstaff family and John Archer had been glad of her help but the men in charge of the bank would take a very dim view of her initiative. Danny had broken in on the orders of Simeon Pemberton, who was desperate to find a reason to dismiss her, and the doorman's confession had shown Harry she needed to cover her tracks more thoroughly. The true correspondence she had exchanged with Esme Longstaff and Archer was no longer kept in her office, but safely hidden away at home. Anyone who went rifling through the filing cabinets that contained the original letters would find the same standard response Harry sent to every other supplication received – that Mr Holmes had retired to Sussex, where he now kept bees. Even so, she set a hair in place when she left the office each day. She was confident that Danny himself would not attempt another break-in but it would be interesting to see if anyone else did.

She had been settled at her desk for perhaps an hour when the faint squeak of a wheel in the corridor heralded the arrival of Bobby. He rapped on the door, poking his head inside when she called out a greeting. 'Got a bumper post bag for you today, Miss White. It seems Christmas is quite the time for murder and whatnot.'

'Alleged murder,' Harry corrected, not quite able to hide a smile at his irrepressible conviction that every letter written to Holmes concerned a real crime. 'But I imagine it's simply that people have more time on their hands and let their imaginations run riot.'

Bobby sighed as he retrieved several thickly bundled packages of envelopes from the brass trolley and handed them to Harry. 'You must wonder about some of them.'

This was a well-worn conversation and one Harry was always at pains to nip in the bud. She liked Bobby immensely but she couldn't afford for him to hit upon anything close to the truth. 'As I have pointed out more than once, these letters are written by people who believe Sherlock Holmes is a living detective who will answer their cry for help. They may not have the strongest grip on what is real and what is not.'

She felt a twinge of guilt as she spoke. While it was true that the majority of the letters were far-fetched and fanciful, she had never felt inclined to laugh or poke fun at those who had written them. In some cases, Holmes was appealed to as a last resort, when the police had failed to show an interest, or procure a satisfactory solution. In others, as in the case of John Archer and his unfortunate uncle, a more discreet investigation was sought. And notwithstanding the detective's fictional status, Harry could almost understand the reasoning that drove so many people to write to him. Sherlock Holmes had an impressive success rate. Nothing got past his gimlet gaze. But there was another reason that ensured Harry treated every letter with respect and compassion. It was that she herself had bought into the pretence that Holmes was real, when she had replied to Esme Longstaff and John Archer, and agreed to investigate the mysteries they laid out before her.

Bobby sniffed. 'They can't all be loopy. I bet there are more crimes going unpunished than you'd think.' He nodded at the bundles of letters. 'It's a shame Sherlock Holmes don't exist. He'd make a fortune out of that lot.'

In the stories, Holmes had never been motivated by money, often charging a minimal fee or sometimes nothing at all. Harry had followed his example, refusing payment for her own investigative efforts. To do otherwise would have felt very wrong. But once again, Bobby's innocent musings were scratching at a door she needed to keep firmly locked. She fixed him with an apologetic smile. 'I'm afraid I really should get on. Was there anything else?'

As ever, he didn't seem to take the dismissal personally. 'Fair enough, Miss White. See you tomorrow, I expect.'

Once he had gone, Harry turned her attention back to her typewriter and continued with the tedious work of typing the same letter she had produced so many times before. She tried not to think about the cluster of envelopes Bobby had left for her. The job was never ending, a mind-numbingly dull task that would surely have driven even the legendary Sisyphus to throw up his hands in despair. But that had been Simeon Pemberton's goal. He couldn't have sacked Harry without the danger of a scandal, so his revenge had been relegation to a role she would find intolerable. But Harry's doll-like appearance hid a steel spine, something Pemberton might have suspected had he been aware of Harry's true status in life. The Abinger family motto was SUIS STAT VIRIBUS – 'He stands by his own strength' – and she had always been taught to hold her ground when it mattered. The fact that she had not been the only victim of Pemberton's lustful nature only made Harry more determined not to show any sign of dissatisfaction with her work. Tea helped, as did a selection of excellent biscuits from Fortnum and Mason, and the occasional deviation from the standard reply to the letters she read. It was a little depressing that Oliver had made her promise not to do so again.

The rest of her working day passed without incident. She took her lunch break in Regent's Park, enjoying the faded blue skies above the spindle-fingered trees in spite of the bitter chill in the air. When it was time to go home, she set her trap in the frame of the door and made her way to Baker Street. The temperature had fallen along with dusk; people hurried along the darkening pavements, heads down against the wintry wind. Few paused at the newspaper sellers but their cries rang out in an effort to tempt them. 'Read all about it! Priceless diamond stolen from locked room. Read all about it!'

Harry almost stopped in her tracks, which caused irritated exclamations to ring out behind her. She ignored the muttered complaints, staring at the newspaper board upon which the headline was emblazoned in bold black print. 'I wonder,' she muttered, frowning as she rummaged in her purse for a coin to pay the seller. A moment later, she stood in the lee of the nearest building, squinting at the newsprint with avid interest. It was exactly as the headline proclaimed – the priceless Sora-Sora diamond had been stolen from a seemingly locked room in a Mayfair town house. The theft had been discovered that morning and the police were said to be baffled. Harry read the entire article twice, then lowered the newspaper, staring absently at the trundling traffic. Could this be the impossible crime referred to in Moriarty's advertisement in yesterday's edition of *The Times*? Was there a chance it might be a serious challenge after all?

2

The first thing Harry did upon reaching the sanctuary of her apartment was to remove her hat and coat and stow them neatly, ready for the morning. She set the kettle on the hob to boil, then took out the clipping she had snipped from the newspaper before leaving Abinger Hall that morning. It had been sandwiched between the pages of the Dorothy L. Sayers novel she was reading and she had all but forgotten it was there until she had seen the jewel theft headlines. Now she read it again, seeking a hidden meaning or subtle clue that would tell her whether she was leaping to a fantastical conclusion rather than assessing the facts. According to Conan Doyle, Moriarty was fond of the occasional chess reference or cypher but if there was a secret message in this real-life challenge to Holmes, Harry could not discern it. Frustrated at her own dim-wittedness, she set about lighting the fire. The apartment had been empty since before Christmas and a musty chill hung in the air, causing the living room to feel drab and unwelcoming after the warmth of Abinger Hall's many fireplaces. Of course, that household was managed by an army of domestic staff and

Harry had no one but herself. Perhaps she ought to look into taking on a maid, someone who could visit daily and undertake the small housekeeping tasks Harry herself found it difficult to fit in around her working life, but it seemed awfully extravagant when it was only her. She couldn't offer accommodation, either, so it would need to be a local girl. And what would she think of an employer who kept drab clothes and down-at-heel shoes under the bed in case they needed to disguise themselves? Harry shook her head. The risk was too great. She would simply have to put up with laying the fire and changing the bedlinen herself.

Once the tinder had begun to crackle in the fireplace, Harry turned her attention to another necessary comfort: the kettle had begun to whistle. Using a little of the boiling water to warm the teapot, she set the tray. But no sooner had she measured the tea leaves into the pot than the telephone rang.

'Mayfair 831,' she said into the receiver.

'Have you seen the evening headlines?'

The clipped voice belonged to Oliver and he did not sound pleased. Harry didn't need him to elaborate. 'The diamond theft. Yes, I saw it. Do you think it's connected to Moriarty's letter?'

He grunted. 'It's certainly an impossible crime. I've spoken to a contact at Scotland Yard and they have no idea how the theft happened. The room was locked, there was a guard on the door to ensure no one went in or out, and the safe is the latest top-of-the-range model from Compton and Wendell – installed last year, secreted in the wall and supposedly unbreakable.'

Harry recalled the front page, which had been full of sensation but scant on detail. The Sora-Sora gemstone was an exceptionally rare red diamond – one of only ten or so in the known world – and currently occupied pride of place in a magnificent, many-jewelled tiara belonging to the Crown Prince of Rangier. Its presence in the Berkeley Square house was perhaps the most baffling thing of all: the prince and his wife were visiting London ahead of a state dinner with His Majesty King George V but they had been widely reported as occupying the lavish Royal Suite at the Savoy Hotel. Harry could understand why such a precious item might not have been entrusted to the hotel's safety deposit box but the Savoy was only a stone's throw from Coutts Bank on the Strand, where she assumed Crown Prince Rupert must have an account. How had the Sora-Sora diamond come to be in a private residence in the first place?

'The house belongs to Lord Delaware,' Oliver said, when Harry voiced her puzzlement. 'He was a diplomatic attaché to Rangier for years and apparently became firm friends with the Crown Prince. I imagine that has something to do with it but I don't know more at present.'

Harry nibbled thoughtfully at her lip. Just north of Piccadilly, Berkeley Square sat in the heart of Mayfair. Its four rows were made up of a mixture of grand town houses, newer apartments blocks and discreet businesses, all of which faced onto the leafy, oval-shaped public gardens. It was an extremely desirable address, traditionally occupied by the wealthiest of residents, and she was sure there were plenty of valuables stored within the properties overlooking the elegant gardens. It wasn't a surprise that there should be a heavy-duty safe in Lord Delaware's house but it was astonishing that a priceless royal diamond should be stored there. 'I assume the household staff are under suspicion,' she said.

'Naturally,' Oliver replied. 'But Lord Delaware is adamant they knew nothing of what was being kept in the safe. Prince Rupert's own man sat guarding the door and only Delaware held the key. Yet when he and the guard unlocked the door to retrieve the tiara, the safe lay open and the Sora-Sora diamond was missing.'

'Only the diamond?' Harry pressed. 'Not the entire tiara?'

'Apparently not,' Oliver said. 'Which is remarkable in itself.'

'Remarkable indeed,' she mused. 'What kind of thief goes to so much trouble and only takes one jewel?'

He caught her meaning, as she knew he would. 'One who knows exactly what they want,' he said dryly. 'But it could be a coincidence.'

'It's a classic locked-room mystery,' Harry pointed out. 'What better way to catch the eye of the world's greatest detective?'

'You may be right but it doesn't actually matter. Impossible crime or not, it's in the hands of the police now.'

Harry swallowed a sigh. She'd known this would be his position. As a lawyer, Oliver dealt in facts and evidence and certainties. He had no time for gut feelings or intuition. 'Then why did you call me?'

Now it was Oliver's turn to sigh. 'Because I know you, Harry. I wanted to make sure you weren't about to hare off to the scene of the crime.'

She shifted uncomfortably. Berkeley Square was no distance at all from Hamilton Square – it would only take her a few minutes to walk there. 'So what if I am? There's no law against it.'

'No, there isn't,' he said, and she could picture him frowning. 'But with the greatest respect, this is not your business, Harry. As a lawyer and your friend, I advise you in the strongest terms to let Scotland Yard handle it.'

The worst of it was, she knew he was right. The cases she had investigated so far had involved serious crimes but they had not been under investigation by the police. Meddling in the business of Scotland Yard was something Sherlock Holmes did all the time but Harry did not have the same freedom. 'Has anyone ever told you you're no fun, Oliver Fortescue?'

'One or two people,' he conceded. 'But I can live with that if it prevents you from taking unnecessary risks.'

He certainly erred on the side of caution, Harry thought as she recalled how often he had frowned over her recklessness since she'd first asked for his help. But he had also knelt at her side in a rat-infested hovel, kept her role in foiling a criminal gang from the police, and stood by her side knee-deep in freezing fen water as they eavesdropped on unseen enemies. On each occasion, she'd been very glad of his company. 'You are an excellent lawyer and friend,' she replied, ignoring the sudden warmth in her cheeks. 'Your advice is always welcome.'

Oliver snorted. 'I doubt that. But I like to think it's worth listening to.'

Harry pondered the conversation for some time after saying goodbye, turning the peculiarities of the crime over and over. No matter how hard she tried to disassociate the theft of the diamond from the advertisement in the agony column of *The Times*, she couldn't shake the feeling that someone had gone to a lot of trouble to create the perfect opening of a Sherlock Holmes adventure. Holmes himself might acknowledge that such a coincidence was possible, but he would satisfy his mind one way or the other by examining the data, and Harry was forced to admit she did not have a shred of evidence there was any connection between the stolen diamond and Moriarty's letter. There was one thing of which she was certain, however. It would not hurt to keep a watchful eye on the investigation at Berkeley Square.

* * *

Quaglino's restaurant, tucked away beneath the St James's Palace Hotel on Bury Street, would not have been Harry's first choice for a discreet conversation about a delicate family matter. Famed as a place to see and be seen, it was frequented by a glitzy crowd – darlings of radio and stage, artistic types with fashionably loose morals and, of course, the very wealthy. Lord Mountbatten was a regular, along with his wife Edwina, despite scandalous rumours of her affair with the bar's much-vaunted singer. It was one of Seb's favourite haunts, so Harry wasn't especially surprised when he suggested it for dinner that evening, but he had been at pains to reassure her it would be quiet. 'Nothing gets going until eleven o'clock at the earliest. You'll be home long before things get wild.'

'Then why not go to Brownings?' she had asked, thinking of the old-fashioned booths and discreet service the restaurant offered.

'Because the menu is dull and the clientele is even duller,' Seb replied. 'It's a ghastly business poking around in a sibling's *affaire de coeur*, but I don't see why we can't take the sting out of it with some decent oysters.'

Harry couldn't argue with that. She knew very little about the woman their youngest brother had become involved with, other than their mother's fear that she was more interested in his allowance than his affections, but the fact that the alarm had been raised was not a good sign. 'I want to be in bed by ten o'clock at the latest,' she'd warned Seb. 'I have work in the morning.'

'Of course,' Seb had responded dryly. 'I wouldn't want to deprive the bank of its most over-qualified secretary. Entire fortunes might fall.'

It was a source of considerable bemusement among Harry's family members that she had a job at all. When she had first voiced her intention to work in London, her mother had been nonplussed. 'But you don't need to earn money, darling. You have everything you need here.'

On the surface that was true and Harry was well aware of the privileged life she had been born into. The granddaughter of a baron, who would in the fullness of time become the daughter of a baron, might indulge in charitable work but she was not expected to enter paid employment. And while there were many worthy causes to choose from, Harry found herself chafing at the restrictions of both her class and sex. She wanted to do more than attend charity luncheons and make polite conversation with women who moved in the same stultifying social circles as everyone else Harry knew. She dreamed of independence, the freedom to make at least some choices for herself, to stretch her wings a little. Eventually, her parents had given in to her steadfast determination and agreed to an apartment in the right part of London. Lawrence and Seb had been tasked with keeping a brotherly eye on her but, as Seb had once remarked, she was so boring that she made the Archbishop of Canterbury look Bohemian and they mostly left her alone, which was exactly the way Harry liked it. 'Ha ha,' she said to Seb. 'Pick me up at seven-thirty.'

Quaglino's was busy, even for a Tuesday, which was a testament to the charm and business savvy of its owner, the eponymous John Quaglino, who greeted every arrival by name and presented female guests with a flower as though they were the most captivating creature he had ever seen. The bar was draped with elegant drinkers, all hopeful of securing a table before the night's festivities got underway, while a saxophone solo soared from the band tucked away in one corner. Harry and Seb were seated at a table among the other well-dressed diners, where white-suited waiters danced attendance upon their every whim, and Harry wasn't surprised to note that her brother seemed to know everyone. 'That's the novelist Aubrey Wells over there, with his mistress, Gertrude King,' he said, flicking his gaze between the tables. 'It appears Beatrice Barber has given her awful husband the slip once again. And goodness, Lord and Lady Furness are dining together in public. The Prince of Wales must have given her the night off.'

It was common knowledge in elevated circles that Thelma Furness was Edward's mistress, meaning Harry always felt a little sorry for her husband. He did not look happy now, but nor did Thelma. Neither appeared to have much to say. Harry turned a stern eye upon her brother. 'You really are a terrible gossip.'

Seb raised an eyebrow. 'On the contrary, I'm a terribly good gossip. What I don't enjoy is being the subject of other people's tittle-tattle. Which brings us neatly onto our dear brother and his paramour, the delightfully named Serafina Eccleston.'

Harry took a sip of champagne. Holmes would undoubtedly deduce purely from her name where in the country the girl was from, and what her parents' occupation had been, but it meant little to Harry. 'I don't think I know her. Where did they meet? More importantly, when did they meet? Rufus has been in the wilds of Scotland for months.'

'Excellent questions,' Seb replied. 'I'd be very surprised if you did know Miss Eccleston, given you never venture into Soho, but it seems she was part of the reason for sending Rufus away in the first place. You recall the unfortunate night he was arrested in Piccadilly?'

Harry did, although she hadn't witnessed his drunken antics for herself. She'd heard about it from Oliver, who had been summoned to the police station in order to smooth things over. 'Yes.'

'Once Fortescue had arranged his release, he took him to Lawrence, who demanded to know what the blazes he'd been thinking and the truth came tumbling out.'

'I thought they'd been drinking in a nightclub and someone had dared him to climb the statue of Eros,' she said, frowning.

'Which appears to be what happened,' Seb agreed. 'But the reason he took the dare was to impress a young lady. Enter Miss Serafina Eccleston, a beauty of unparalleled grace and goodness with whom Rufus declared himself to be helplessly and eternally in love.'

'Ah,' Harry said, as the pieces began to fall into place.

'The following morning, he announced that he planned to propose to her,' Seb went on. 'Unable to get much information out of Rufus, beyond descriptions of lustrous hair and shimmering eyes, Lawrence decided to approach the friends he had been drinking with. One of them revealed she is a dance hostess at the Hot Spot Club on Gerrard Street. That's where she met Rufus, some weeks earlier.'

Harry felt her heart sink. While she'd never visited any of the many nightclubs that seemed to spring up and close virtually overnight in Soho, she'd read enough reports of police raids in the newspapers to know the role of a hostess involved much more than encouraging the clientele to dance along to the band. Often unlicensed, the clubs were run as bottle parties, which allowed them to serve alcohol past legal hours. Guests were required to sign an 'invitation' to gain entry, and place a private order for the drinks they wanted to consume while on the premises, usually at ridiculously high prices. The job of a hostess was to encourage them to stay longer and drink more, and perhaps lure them into worse vices. It was not, Harry thought, an encouraging discovery.

'As you'd expect, Lawrence reported this to Mama and Papa,

who confronted Rufus and made it clear that an engagement was out of the question,' Seb continued. 'He refused to break things off and was immediately sent to contemplate his choices in the Highlands.'

The change had done Rufus good, Harry had thought when he'd returned to Abinger Hall for Christmas. Gone was the slightly sallow tinge brought about by too many late nights – he'd been clear-eyed and straight-backed, glowing with the kind of good health only fresh air and exercise could provide. She even thought he'd grown an inch, so that he was almost as tall as Seb. His demeanour had changed too – he had always been mercurial, charming one moment and furious the next, but he'd been agreeable and polite throughout the holiday. Perhaps suspiciously so, Harry mused now. 'Let me guess – he didn't break things off with Miss Eccleston.'

Seb sighed. 'He did not. Great-Uncle Douglas mentioned to Mama that Rufus had received a number of letters from London while he'd been in Scotland. He forwarded one that had arrived after Rufus had left, which she intercepted and read.'

Harry winced, caught between indignation that their mother would do such a thing and apprehension about what the letter revealed. 'And?'

'Rather than return to Great-Uncle Douglas at the end of this week, it seems Rufus plans to elope to Gretna Green with Miss Eccleston, where they will be married over the blacksmith's anvil. The letter details which train she will be taking and reminds him to bring money for lodgings on their wedding night.'

Harry groaned. None of them had met Serafina Eccleston and it was possible they were doing both her and Rufus a great disservice. The two of them could very well be a pair of star-crossed lovers and their desperate plans to elope the result of being denied a more leisurely courtship. But the speed with which matters were moving troubled Harry. There was a strong possibility that her mother was right, that Miss Eccleston was trying to improve her situation in life and she had chosen Rufus as the means to do so. 'What happens now?'

'Obviously, Mama has invented a reason not to send Rufus back to Scotland as planned,' Seb said. 'And she's tasked me and Lawrence with finding a way to persuade Serafina to break things off. I suppose we'll have to pay her.'

'I suppose so,' Harry echoed doubtfully. She had no idea how much it would cost to satisfy the girl – it all depended how confident she was of her beau's affections. Rufus was not in line to inherit anything more than a sizeable allowance, but he did offer status and a very nice lifestyle. That could be worth more to a determined gold digger than a quick pay-off. And there was also a chance she was truly in love with Rufus, in which case Harry assumed no amount of money would deter her. The trouble was that while an indignant refusal might be terribly romantic, it wouldn't overcome the fundamental difficulty of her station in life. Evelyn White might say she wanted her children to have happy, loving marriages, but Harry did not imagine that extended to welcoming a dance hostess into the family, no matter how anguished Rufus became. If it was love, he would need the support of his brothers and sisters to overcome their mother's objections, and none of them could offer that without a better understanding of who Miss Eccleston was. 'Do you think we should find out a little more about her before we jump to any conclusions?'

'How?' Seb asked, looking askance. 'No crime has been committed, as far as we know, so we can't trouble the police. Surely you're not suggesting we hire a detective?'

Endeavouring to maintain a neutral expression, Harry waved a dismissive hand. 'Of course not. But some discreet enquiries might be prudent. We might uncover something we can use.'

He cocked his head. 'You've been reading too many mystery novels.'

'Probably,' she said, forcing herself to smile.

'Still, you might have a point,' Seb mused. 'As the great Sun Tzu said, attack is the secret of defence. I'll speak to Fortescue, see what he thinks. He might know someone at Scotland Yard who can do a bit of digging around on the sly.'

'Oh, do you think so?' Harry said, wrinkling her forehead as though the idea would never have occurred to her. 'Yes, I suppose he might.'

'In fact, I'm going to delegate that task to you, Harry,' Seb said, beaming at her in self-satisfaction. 'The two of you can discuss it over dinner or drinks – it might be just the nudge he needs to see you as more than Lawrence's little sister, eh?'

Given Oliver's involvement in Harry's recent adventures as R. K. Moss, she was fairly certain that his opinion of her had already undergone some extensive changes, even if he hadn't expressly said so. When she had first sought his help, to visit Mildred Longstaff in Holloway Prison several months earlier, he had agreed out of duty to Lawrence but hadn't backed away when Harry admitted the truth about her interest in Mildred's plight. Despite clear reservations, he had continued to assist and, on more than one occasion since, Harry had caught him observing her with what looked very much like respect, which suggested he had learned she was considerably more capable than she might appear. Perhaps he was even beginning to regard her as an equal, a thought that gave her no small amount of satisfaction; her own opinion of him had certainly deepened in return. But Seb didn't need to know that she and Oliver had developed a partnership that was quite separate from his friendliness with Lawrence. Apart from anything else, it suited Harry to pretend Oliver might use an acquaintance at Scotland Yard to look into Miss Eccleston. It meant she could employ agents of her own, without having to explain how she had come by the information. 'An excellent idea,' she said. 'I'll speak to him tomorrow.'

'I recommend Gordon's Wine Bar, near Charing Cross,' Seb offered, raising his champagne glass with a suggestive wink. 'Full of nooks and crannies for secluded tête-à-têtes.'

He really was incorrigible, Harry thought with exasperation. The teenage crush she'd once nursed for Oliver was a thing of the distant past, but Seb rarely missed an opportunity to tease her about it and the teasing was made all the more annoying by the fact that her heart still felt the occasional flutter when her guard was down. It was something she would rather die than admit but she supposed it wouldn't do any harm for any onlookers to mistake them for a couple, especially since Oliver had no idea how she had once felt. 'Thanks for the tip,' she managed, with only a hint of asperity.

Her dryness was lost on Seb. 'Let me know what he uncovers,' he replied, and was instantly distracted by the approach of their waiter. 'And look – here are the oysters. Now the evening can really get going.'

3

It was a little before midday on Wednesday when Harry discovered the letter from Esme Longstaff. The envelope was addressed in the same copperplate handwriting Harry recognised from the young woman's previous correspondence, although one or two of the vowels were carelessly shaped, as though written in haste. Frowning, Harry slit the envelope apart and withdrew the letter.

Mr Sherlock Holmes
221b Baker Street
London
NW1 6XE

5, The Cottages
Foxley
Surrey

23 December 1932

Dear Mr Holmes

Please forgive me for intruding upon you once more, and with a matter I am by no means certain is worthy of your attention. But having begun, I must go forward and allow you to be the judge of the strange and puzzling encounter my father experienced when returning from London by train last evening.

He was, by his own admission, in peculiar spirits. The journey into London was due to an interview for a position with Marshall and Sons on Tooley Street, but when he presented himself, the company had no record of having invited him. Left with no option but to return to Waterloo station, he took the next train home. He was joined in his compartment by a stranger, who seemed in some agitation, muttering and wringing his hands until my father was obliged to ask if he was quite well. The stranger apologised for his behaviour and introduced himself as Mr Spender. They shook hands and the man lapsed into silence, although it appeared he could not sit still. When he jumped to his feet for the fourth or fifth time, exclaiming aloud, my father asked whether there was anything he could do to help. The man subsided into the seat once more. 'Would that there were, sir,' he said. 'But I fear it is too late for anyone to intercede now. My poor girl is lost to me.'

Startled, my father asked what he meant. Mr Spender explained that his youngest daughter had vanished in London some weeks earlier and no trace could be found of her. He had spent the day combing the city streets, to no avail. 'I do not know what I shall tell her mother,' he said heavily. 'The disappointment will surely kill her this time.'

I am certain you will understand that my father saw in this stranger a kindred soul, a man suffering the same agony we had endured when my dear sister was missing. When it became apparent that the police had been very little help, he suggested Mr Spender consult a detective. 'We have!' the man cried. 'They take our money and offer no relief. Our Polly remains lost.'

At that, my father was quiet, because he had sworn to tell no one of your involvement in Mildred's case. And yet the other man's distress weighed upon him, until at last the train pulled into the station and he stood to leave. 'There is someone who can find her,' he said, as he opened the door and prepared to step onto the platform. 'Many believe him to be a work of fiction but he helped me and I am certain he could help you. His name is Sherlock Holmes.'

You must believe that he meant no harm, sir. The encounter was so very strange and yet I cannot shake the uneasiness it has provoked in me. On the surface, it appears to be simple serendipity, but I cannot rest. Should you find yourself contacted by this man, perhaps you will be able to reassure me that my anxiety is misplaced. I do hope so.

Yours faithfully

Miss Esme Longstaff

Harry read the letter three times before lowering it to the desk, a deep frown furrowing her brow. She knew of a Polly Spender; a girl with that name had, until recently, been a maid in the household of the wealthy Lord and Lady Finchem. Her sudden departure from that position had troubled Harry, coming only a few weeks after the theft that had seen Mildred Longstaff sacked from the same house, and she suspected Polly knew more about that than she was telling. It was possible she had been involved in some way, perhaps even part of the criminal gang that had later tried to frame Mildred for the much bigger robbery that had seen her sent to Holloway. Could it be the same girl? But that Polly Spender had not been missing in December. Harry's associate, Beth Chamberlain, had tracked the maid down in Southwark and tried to winkle more information from her. The effort failed; Beth reported that Polly had been too afraid of the possible consequences to admit anything. And now, according to the stranger on Mr Longstaff's train, she had disappeared. Could it be Polly's fears had been justified?

Putting aside the question of identity, Harry turned to the peculiar details of the encounter on the train. It was quite a coincidence that Mr Spender had boarded that same train and carriage as Mr Longstaff – a man who had suffered a remarkably similar familial heartache – but made more notable still by the fact that he had only been aboard the train because someone had summoned him to London for a false interview. Could it have been a ruse to ensure he would be in a certain place at a certain time? It might even be reasonably predicted that he would take the next train home after his frustrating visit to Tooley Street. All Mr Spender would need to do was note which carriage he entered and follow. What Harry couldn't comprehend was why he should go to such trouble, especially when there had been no indication he had known who Mr Longstaff was. It was all so strange and yet she was certain Esme's misgivings were well founded. All was not as it seemed.

Rousing herself, Harry reached for a sheet of paper and wrote a hasty note to Beth. Satisfied that her instructions were plain, she addressed an envelope and sealed it, ready for posting. That done, she lifted the telephone receiver to call Oliver. After a brief explanation, she donned her hat and coat, and scooped up the letter to Beth. She could only hope the queue in the post office would be short.

* * *

Oliver was waiting in Cavendish Square when Harry arrived just after one o'clock. He was seated at one of the benches lining the outer path, muffled against the cold in a heavy overcoat and hat, reading a newspaper. Blackbirds cawed from the leafless trees as weak January sunlight did its best to dispel the winter gloom. She made her way quickly towards him, dodging pedestrians and prams, conscious that she had used almost half of her lunch break already.

'Thank you for coming,' she said, perching on the chilly wood beside him.

Oliver lowered the newspaper. 'Unfortunately, I don't have long. Did you bring Miss Longstaff's letter?'

Withdrawing it from her bag, Harry laid it on the bench. 'I have no idea what it means.'

He took the envelope, exchanging it for his now folded copy of that morning's *The Times*. 'Meanwhile, someone is growing impatient.' He tapped the front page. 'It appears the game is not yet afoot.'

With a blink of surprise, Harry took up the broadsheet, scanning the lines of personal advertisements that made up the extensive agony column. Sandwiched between an appeal for unwanted false teeth and an advertisement for Cuthbert's Travelling Circus, she found the one bearing a familiar name.

> My dear Sherlock Holmes, I confess myself disappointed. *Tempus fugit.* Yours in expectation, Professor James Moriarty

Harry had not enjoyed Latin at school but she had retained enough to translate *Tempus fugit* into 'Time flies'. It was exactly the kind of message Moriarty might send. Whoever was placing the advertisements must know the character well. What they were trying to achieve was less clear.

Oliver had turned his attention to Esme's letter. 'I suppose the first question must concern the desperate Mr Spender,' he said, once he reached the end. 'Has he written to Holmes to beg his help?'

Harry shook her head. She had opened every letter from the Christmas backlog. There had been the usual assortment of petty concerns regarding neighbours and libellous accusations of worse crimes, along with one or two accounts that Harry imagined might have inspired Sir Arthur Conan Doyle to put pen to paper, but there was nothing from a Mr Spender, nor were any of the letters a plea for help to locate a missing young woman. 'Not yet.'

'I could make some discreet enquiries,' he said, pursing his lips. 'If Polly's father has reported her disappearance to the police then there will be a report.'

'If?' Harry echoed, and gave him a measured look. 'You don't believe his story.'

'It may all be exactly as he describes,' Oliver said. 'In which case the police will have made every effort to find his daughter and those efforts will be documented. We'll be able to set Miss Longstaff's mind at rest on that score, at least. But if no report has been made, we are left with several pressing questions.'

She nodded. 'Firstly, who set up the false interview to get Mr Longstaff to London? I think we may assume they are connected to Mr Spender in some way.'

'It could be someone at Marshall and Sons. But an official-looking letter on headed paper could be mocked up by any half-skilled forger so I don't think we can wholly suspect them.'

'Then we come to Mr Spender himself,' Harry went on. 'It seems clear that he entered Mr Longstaff's carriage with a purpose. If Polly is missing, then I suppose it's possible he sought the name of the person who had helped to find Mildred.'

'Then why not simply ask?' Oliver said.

'Perhaps he thought Mr Longstaff would recognise her name,' Harry said but even as she spoke, she realised the suggestion was flawed.

'If that were true, he wouldn't have revealed her name at all.' Oliver pounced, as she knew he would. 'Everything rests on Polly herself. Nothing will become clear until we discover whether she has truly disappeared. I'll see what I can find out.'

'I've asked Beth to put some feelers out too. She might get quicker results.'

Oliver's gaze sharpened. 'I'm not sure that's wise. If there is a link between Polly's possible disappearance and Mildred, then we know what kind of people we're dealing with.'

His words gave Harry a momentary flicker of doubt. Was she putting Beth in danger by asking her to see what she could find out? 'Beth is smart,' she said, reminding herself how capable and resourceful the other woman had proved so far. 'She'll be careful.'

'I hope so.' He nodded at the newspaper. 'What do you make of that?'

Harry pursed her lips. 'If it is a game between friends then one party doesn't seem to be playing along. But if the impossible crime is the theft of the diamond then why challenge anyone to solve it? Why not simply vanish?'

'Oh, I'm certain it is a game,' Oliver said. 'The question is, who is it against?'

'Exactly,' Harry agreed. 'Why Holmes? Why not a real detective – one of your friends at Scotland Yard?'

He drummed his fingers on the wooden seat. 'I haven't read

a great number of Sherlock Holmes stories but I seem to recall that Moriarty is described as the shadowy mastermind behind any number of underworld gangs. The two cases you've investigated have both turned out to be cogs in a larger criminal organisation. It's possible those investigations have been noticed.'

Harry considered what she knew about London's lawless gangs. According to the newspaper reports, most favoured a more smash-and-grab approach to conducting their business. They did not set elaborate traps for those who foiled their plans. 'I suppose that's a possibility. But it's quite a leap to trace things back to Sherlock Holmes. Apart from anything else, no one knows he was even consulted.'

'No one except the Longstaffs and John Archer,' Oliver corrected. He patted Esme's letter. 'And it seems Mr Longstaff cannot keep a secret.'

She stared at him. Could the strange encounter on the train be somehow related to the challenge thrown down to Holmes? It seemed preposterous and yet there was a sort of twisted logic to it that suited Conan Doyle's descriptions of his arch-villain. 'If you're right then someone has gone to a lot of trouble to uncover the truth,' she said slowly, turning the idea over in her mind. 'To uncover the person acting as Holmes.'

Oliver spread his hands. 'As I said, it's a game. And you don't need me to warn you that choosing to play along is high risk.'

A prickle of unease rippled down Harry's spine. The mystery of the missing diamond intrigued her but the idea that an unknown someone might be trying to lure her out from Holmes' shadow was deeply unsettling. 'I have no taste for gambling.'

'Then our path remains unchanged,' Oliver replied, picking

up the newspaper and folding it neatly. 'Once the seven days are up, Moriarty will realise his ploy has failed.'

He was right, of course. All she had to do was ignore the bait. Checking her watch, Harry saw it was nearly time to return to work. 'There is something else I need to talk to you about,' she said, recalling her conversation with Seb the night before. 'Some family business that I won't go into now. Are you free for drinks this evening?'

He cocked his head, his gaze curious. 'Of course. Where did you have in mind?'

'Gordon's, near Charing Cross,' she said, falling back on her brother's suggestion. 'Shall we say seven-thirty?'

'I'll be there,' he said, and the smile he flashed did something peculiar to Harry's insides and temporarily vanquished all thoughts of Mr Spender, the Longstaffs and Moriarty. It was Seb's fault, she decided as she set out at a brisk pace towards Baker Street. His teasing was stirring up old memories, bringing fragments of long-dismissed feelings to the surface and muddying the waters of the clandestine working relationship she and Oliver had forged. But in his defence, Seb was just being Seb; mischievous, meddlesome and entirely unaware that Oliver meant anything more to Harry than a girlish infatuation. And that was the way she intended it to stay.

* * *

Harry's conversation with Oliver weighed heavily upon her for the rest of the afternoon as she worked. She had taken some precautions to hide her own identity while investigating on behalf of Holmes, but she now saw she had not been careful enough. If Moriarty was the mastermind behind the previous cases she had solved, then there was a danger the trail might lead to Harry herself. It was not a cheering thought. What would Holmes do, she pondered as her fingers flew automatically over the typewriter keys. Would he choose to be the mouse in Moriarty's game? Or would he seize the initiative and become the cat? The answer was abundantly clear; he would accept the challenge and track Moriarty down. But Holmes had an advantage Harry did not – he was a fictional character with a benevolent creator to rescue him from impending disaster. She had no such protection and, as Oliver had been at pains to point out, her investigations had already crossed ruthless men and women. But what was it Seb had said the evening before, when discussing the best approach to the problem of Serafina Eccleston? Attack was the secret of defence. If Holmes, and therefore Harry, were in danger, the best defence might be to strike at Moriarty first. The difficulty was that she could only see one move to make. And she was all too aware it was exactly what Moriarty wanted her to do.

4

The first thing Oliver did after greeting Harry at Gordon's Wine Bar that evening was to present her with an envelope. It was addressed to Sarah Smith – another alias Harry had adopted for her undercover work – and had been sent to Oliver's chambers on Lincoln's Inn Fields. Harry recognised Beth's handwriting immediately, although she hadn't expected a reply by return.

'Trouble?' Oliver asked, as she scanned the letter inside.

'Information,' Harry replied absently, frowning as she read. Reaching the end, she looked up. 'Tell me, did you have time to contact anyone at Scotland Yard about Polly Spender?'

Oliver poured her a glass of ruby-red wine from the bottle already on the table. 'I did, but they haven't come back to me yet. A lot of their resources are being used at Berkeley Square. Why?'

Folding the letter, Harry returned it to the envelope. 'Beth took a trip to Southwark this afternoon and she says Polly Spender hasn't been home for almost a week. No one seems to know where she is. The rumour is she's working.'

Oliver lifted an eyebrow. 'I assume you don't mean as a maid.'

'Beth wasn't able to find out,' Harry said. 'But that's not the most interesting part. Mr Spender is also away from home at the moment.'

'Ah,' Oliver said. 'Did Beth manage to find out where he is?'

Harry nodded. 'He was found guilty of petty theft last November. He's been in Wandsworth Prison ever since.'

He stared at her. 'That is interesting. So who exactly did Mr Longstaff meet on the train?'

'A very good question. But it wasn't the father of our Polly Spender. It would be helpful to establish whether there are two girls with the same name.'

'Of course,' Oliver said. 'I'll pursue it in the morning.'

Sitting back in her chair, Harry took a moment to absorb their surroundings. The wine bar was below ground, occupying what she assumed had once been the cellar. Low vaulted ceilings stretched over their heads, lit only by the amber glow of candlelight. The tables had been spaced far enough apart to give those seated at them a little privacy as they talked, although the alcoves cut into the walls were the most secluded. These were draped with crimson velvet curtains and Harry could only catch glimpses of those sitting behind. She could see why her brother had described the atmosphere as romantic – the lighting alone was designed to encourage a multitude of sins – and she couldn't help wondering how many scandalous liaisons the waiters turned a blind eye towards every night. But she was here to discuss Rufus and his unfortunate attachment to Serafina Eccleston, not pass judgement on the love affairs of strangers. She would leave that to Seb.

'Investigating Polly's whereabouts wasn't the only task I asked Beth to undertake,' she said, turning her attention back to Oliver. 'There's no easy way to say this. I'm afraid Rufus has got himself into something of a situation – one that requires delicate handling.'

He did not look surprised. 'Again?'

Harry dipped her head. 'He does have a talent for it. Regrettably, his actions are a little more far-reaching this time. It began the evening you rescued him from the police station.'

He listened as she relayed everything Seb had told her two nights previously. When she had finished, Oliver was quiet for a moment. 'I can certainly check whether Miss Eccleston is known to the police. I assume Beth's second task was something similar.'

'Yes, although I confess I have no idea how she will manage it. Investigating Polly was simpler – Beth was already acquainted with her and knew something of her background.' She paused. 'I did wonder if I should meet Serafina for myself.'

The look he gave her was measured. 'By visiting the Hot Spot, you mean? I'm not sure it's your scene.'

If even half of the lurid stories featured in the newspapers were true, then Harry had to agree that a Soho nightclub was no place for a respectable young woman. But it wasn't the first time Oliver had suggested there were places she shouldn't visit. She thought he might know better by now. 'Maybe not but I can't think of another way to get the measure of her.'

For a moment, she thought he might argue, but he appeared to notice the mulish set of her jaw. 'I don't recommend you go alone.'

Harry raised her chin. 'I won't. I thought Beth and I might go together – two fashionable young things looking to let their hair down a little.'

'I meant you ought to take a man with you,' he said. 'Obviously, I can't go, for professional reasons, but I'm sure Seb would be amenable, if you asked him. I expect you know he's no stranger to such places.'

Harry had always preferred not to enquire too deeply into the details of her brother's social life, on the grounds that what she didn't know couldn't worry her. And it went without saying that she would not dream of asking Oliver to take such a risk. His standing as a lawyer had to remain beyond reproach. 'Seb is the obvious choice,' she said. 'But how would I find out anything important with him there? He'd simply get in the way.'

Oliver eyed her solemnly. 'You can't go alone, Harry. I'm well aware that you can handle yourself, and I imagine your friend Beth knows a thing or two about the seedier side of London nightlife, but you're going to have to trust me. Going somewhere like the Hot Spot without a male chaperone would be a mistake.'

Indignation fired in her belly and it took a monumental effort of will to quell it. His use of the word 'chaperone' did not help – it harkened back to the Victorian era, when women could be considered ruined for even entering the places men were free to go whenever they pleased. But it was also possible – even likely – that she and Beth might attract some unwanted attention. Perhaps Oliver had a point. 'I suppose Seb can't very well refuse to take me, since it's for the good of our baby brother. Perhaps Beth can do the digging while I distract him with drink.'

Oliver's mouth twitched. 'I imagine that would work. But I agree that it complicates things. How will you explain her to him, and vice versa, without giving your secrets away to both?'

It was another excellent point. Beth had worked out for herself that Harry was not who she pretended to be, but she had no idea of her true identity. And presenting Beth to Seb as a new friend would raise more questions than it answered. Oliver was right – it was a complication. 'I'll think of something.'

'I have no doubt you will,' he replied, evidently resigning himself to the inevitable. 'When will you go? I assume time is of the essence.'

Harry considered the temperament of her youngest brother, whose plans had already been thwarted once. No doubt he was feverishly plotting another way to escape from Abinger Hall to elope with his beloved. 'It rather depends on whether I can persuade Seb,' she said. 'Tomorrow night, if he agrees, or perhaps Friday.'

Oliver eyed her across the table. 'I'd like you to promise you won't go without him. I know you're worried about Rufus but there are other ways to investigate Miss Eccleston that don't put your safety and reputation in danger.' Harry opened her mouth to speak but he held up a hand. 'And I know you think I'm too cautious and monstrously dull, but I've prosecuted several proprietors of these places and believe me, some of the things that go on behind the scenes would shock you. If you must go, at least be sensible about it.'

She stared at him in silent frustration. Of course he had guessed that she would visit the Hot Spot with or without her brother. Nor was he wrong that his careful approach had driven her to distraction on more than one occasion during their adventures. But she had also come to respect his opinion and she had to concede that his experience of London's nightlife was greater than her own, even if he'd never actually set foot in an illegal club. 'I don't think you're monstrously dull.'

His lips quirked. 'Thank you. But do I have your word?'

Harry sighed. 'Yes, Oliver, you have my word.'

'Good,' he said, and hesitated. 'And I hope you know that

I'm not trying to hold you back. I only have your best interests at heart.'

His dark eyes appeared fathomless in the shadows cast by the candles, fixed upon her. Harry fought the urge to fall into their depths, reminding herself yet again that his intentions towards her were those of a trusted family friend. In protecting her, he was guarding the Abinger name and reputation. 'Of course I do,' she said, and reached for her wine glass. 'And I'd like to point out that I do listen to you. I haven't poked my nose into the Berkeley Square theft, have I?'

Oliver shook his head. 'You forget that I'm a lawyer, Harry. I'm trained to notice the things my clients aren't saying. And the word missing from that sentence is *yet*.'

She took a sip of her drink, galled that he'd divined her intentions again. 'Have the police made any progress? I don't imagine Prince Rupert is a patient man and he has friends in high places.'

'The highest,' Oliver agreed. 'Scotland Yard is under immense pressure to crack the case but it doesn't appear they have much to go on. No one went into the room and no one came out, and yet the diamond is gone.'

'An impossible crime,' Harry observed, her tone studiously innocent.

He contemplated her for a long moment, then sighed. 'This is going to involve another madcap disguise, isn't it?'

'What a capital suggestion,' she replied, and checked the time. 'How do you feel about a visit to the Garston Club?'

'The Garston?' he echoed, nonplussed. 'Why on earth would I go there? Unless—'

She watched understanding cross his face. The Garston Club was a gentlemen-only establishment not far from the Strand, a venue Harry could not enter for herself. But Oliver was a member and he had met John Archer there when the man had begged for the help of Sherlock Holmes. 'It's possible Mr Archer might be at home in Cambridgeshire, tending to his uncle, but I think it's worth a try. And if he is in London—'

'You want to enlist his help with your disguise,' Oliver finished.

Harry spread her hands. 'Who better to make me unrecognisable than a trained actor, with the whole of the Drury Lane theatre wardrobe at his disposal?'

Oliver gazed broodingly at what was left of his wine. 'And then?'

'And then I visit the scene of the crime to work out how it was done,' she said.

'Just like that,' he said, arching an eyebrow. 'When the finest minds in London's police force have so far failed to find any clues. How do you propose getting inside?'

She beamed at him as she set her empty glass back on the table. 'Elementary, my dear Fortescue. But let's see if Mr Archer is in town first.'

* * *

It seemed to Harry that it took an age for Oliver to reappear in the doorway of the Garston Club. She settled herself on a nearby bench, ignoring the biting chill of the starless January night, and pretended to read her book. As ever, the area was busy but no one troubled her, although she noticed a raggedly dressed girl of around eight or nine eyeing her with professional interest, clearly trying to decide whether she was a worthwhile mark. The timely arrival of a portly bobby on the beat sent the child scurrying before he could approach Harry but she suspected she had not gone far, perhaps loitering in a nearby alleyway until the coast was clear to resume her approach. She hadn't liked the threadbare thinness of the girl's clothes, nor the pinched pallor of her skin. Without haste, she dug into her handbag for a coin and rose, placing the sixpence on the bench as she did so. She did not look back as she trailed in an unhurried fashion after the policeman, trusting that the girl had been watching like a hawk. It was only a little money but perhaps it might get her something to eat.

She took a leisurely stroll along New Row, pausing at regular intervals to glance back towards the Garston to make sure she did not miss Oliver's reappearance. At the junction with St Martin's Lane, she crossed and made her way back along New Row. As she was considering turning into Bedford Street, the door of the Garston Club opened and she saw him emerge. He was not alone.

'My dear Miss Moss, what an unexpected joy!' John Archer exclaimed as he hurried across the road to shake her by the hand. 'I couldn't believe my luck when Mr Fortescue arrived at my table. I had hardly hoped to see you both again so soon.'

His smile was so warm and his greeting so effusive that Harry could not help but forgive him his vigorous pumping of her arm. 'It's good to see you too, Mr Archer. Has Mr Fortescue explained the reason for bothering you?'

Archer spread his arms. 'He has. But it is no trouble at all – I am very happy to help. We can go to the Lane now.'

Harry blinked in surprise. 'Now?'

'Of course. Tonight's performance will be underway, but we can sneak in through the stage door and raid the costume stores in the cellar.' He lowered his voice. 'I assume you are working on behalf of a certain beekeeper?'

The last word was imbued with an especially theatrical flourish which somehow only served to make it more audible.

She nodded. 'An undercover operation of the highest importance,' she confided. 'But I'm afraid that's all we are able to reveal.'

'Naturally,' John Archer said, his eyes twinkling. 'Let's not waste another moment. To the theatre, dear friends!'

The stage door was in Russell Street, a sumptuous red arch that made no attempt at discretion, declaring its presence with a large, unmissable sign. 'But how would our adoring public know where to find us after the performance otherwise?' Archer asked, forehead wrinkling as Harry expressed her surprise.

He tapped at the door. Moments later, one half of the arch was pulled back and a head appeared. 'Oh, it's you, Mr Archer,' the grizzle-bearded man said, then peered at Harry and Oliver. 'Who's this?'

'My esteemed guests,' Archer said grandly. 'We are here to consult Madame Francine. Is she in good spirits this evening?'

The stage door manager bared a set of nicotine-stained teeth in what Harry thought was a grimace of regret. 'Very temperamental, Mr A, it's been a tricky night so far. Miss Greenwood declared her costume had lice and refused to go on for the opening number unless it was fumigated. Mr Selten couldn't find his hat and Madame's new assistant ran into Mr Macklin backstage, brandishing his cane and groaning. She had to take a tot of brandy for her nerves.'

'Ah.' John Archer gave a solemn nod, then turned to Oliver and Harry. 'Perhaps we won't trouble Madame, then. Don't worry, I know exactly where to find what you need.'

Grumbling and muttering, the stage door manager allowed them inside. The corridor beyond the stage door was narrow and dimly lit. The sound of an orchestra in full flow vibrated through the walls as a gaggle of dancers appeared as if from nowhere and vanished along an adjoining passage. 'This way,' Archer said, his usually hearty tone muted as he waved towards a staircase leading downwards. 'We don't want to get tangled up with the production, especially not on a night when Mr Macklin is up to his old tricks.'

Harry exchanged a glance with Oliver. The doorman had mentioned the same name. 'Who is Mr Macklin?'

John Archer gave her a look of mild surprise. 'One of the theatre ghosts. But there's no need for concern – he never ventures into the cellars.'

It wasn't long before Harry found herself in a vaulted cavern for the second time that evening, although this one was lit by flickering overhead bulbs rather than candlelight. Amid the gloom, Harry made out row after row of shapeless rails, each draped with a heavy dust sheet. Clusters of packing crates were dotted here and there, while wooden cupboards lined one long wall, doors closed against the chill. The air was musty with the scent of old fabric, overlain by mothballs and lavender. It reminded Harry a little of home. As a child she and her brothers had played hide-and-seek in the many rooms of Abinger Hall and her grandmother's wardrobes had smelled much the same.

'Behold the cave of wonders,' Archer said, waving an expressive arm that was reflected in an enormous cheval mirror hulking in one corner. 'There's enough magic here to transform you into a Greek goddess or a toothless beggar, Miss Moss. What's it to be?'

With a flourish, he swept the dust sheet from the nearest rail, revealing a riot of colour and finery that dazzled Harry's eyes. Leathery pirate costumes nestled beside brass-buttoned military jackets, gauzy fairy wings peeped out from behind lavish ball gowns and there were at least three bear costumes squashed together at one end. Another rail appeared to be hung with white shirts of differing styles and periods, while a third consisted entirely of men's suits, in various shades of grey, black and brown. Tucked away behind this rail was a vast gilt sarcophagus, resplendent with the face of an imperious bearded pharaoh. Harry dragged her marvelling gaze away from the treasure trove to gaze at John Archer. 'I need you to turn me into a man.'

If Archer was in any way surprised by this, he did not show it. Instead, he turned an enquiring expression towards Oliver. 'And you, Mr Fortescue? A duchess, perhaps?'

Harry fought the urge to giggle. 'He simply needs to look different. I thought perhaps a beard, and a matching wig.'

Oliver gave her a level look. 'You intend me to wear a disguise as well.'

'Naturally. If the scene of the crime is being watched by our adversary, then we need to take steps to conceal both our identities.' She paused, widening her eyes. 'But if you'd rather not then I'm sure I can go without you.'

He opened and closed his mouth, as though formulating and discarding an argument, then sighed. 'Very well. A beard and wig, if you please, Mr Archer.'

The other man nodded. 'Easily done. Are you to be gentlemen of means or working men?'

'Somewhere in between, I think,' Harry said after a moment's consideration. 'Respectable but unremarkable. The sort of men no one really notices.' She thought about the scruffy trousers and flat cap stashed under her bed, worn when she had needed to follow up a lead in Elephant and Castle and just about good enough to fool a casual observer. 'But we need to look convincing under close inspection. Can you help?'

'Hmmm.' Archer scanned the rails of clothing thoughtfully.

'I think we can manage that. A greatcoat and a bowler hat might work for you, Mr Fortescue.' Rustling among the browns and greys, he pulled out a heavy woollen coat and held it towards Oliver, squinting critically. 'Yes, that will do very well.'

Taking the heavy coat, Oliver pulled it on over his suit. Archer crossed to open the first of the cupboards, which Harry saw contained a number of feathered hats and headdresses. The contents of the second cupboard were considerably more mundane; she spotted several top hats, a number of trilbies and a stack of black bowler hats. 'This one should fit,' Archer said, after discarding three or four. 'You'll need to take care not to dislodge your wig if you remove it in polite company.'

A smart pinstripe suit was presented to Harry, complete with waistcoat and pocket handkerchief. 'I fear the trousers will need to be taken up,' Archer said. 'In other circumstances I might have asked Madame Francine to measure you, but I assume discretion is our watchword.'

Harry nodded. 'I can make the adjustments myself. What else do you recommend?'

'Make-up and whiskers,' Archer said, beaming at them both. 'Let me show you how to wield them both to your advantage. I promise you won't recognise yourselves by the time we're finished.'

Thirty minutes later, Harry was forced to agree. Using an old box of stage make-up, John Archer created sunken cheeks where she had none, broadened Oliver's nose so it looked as though it had been flattened in a long-ago fight and added shadows beneath both their eyes, explaining the technique as he went so that they would be able to recreate the effect when needed. Oliver was fitted with a grey wig, along with salt-and-pepper whiskers, and Harry's blonde curls were submerged beneath an unruly black mess of astonishing ugliness. Her upper lip tickled with a bristling dark moustache that felt precariously balanced no matter how much Mr Archer reassured her it would not come off. 'If this glue can endure the heat and toil of the stage, it can survive a cold January day. As long as no one tugs at it, of course.'

Harry eyed her reflection in the age-speckled mirror. Archer had been right – she was almost unrecognisable. Oliver's disguise was equally complete. 'I am Mr Thompson,' she announced gruffly. 'How do you do?'

For a moment, she thought Oliver might baulk, but he inclined his head. 'Mr Gill. Delighted to make your acquaintance.'

Archer glanced back and forth between them in delight. 'Honoured to meet you both, gentlemen. And you may keep the effects for as long as you need them – the current production is set to run until October at the earliest. No one will notice their absence.'

'Thank you,' Harry said, pressing his arm. 'We're in your debt.'

'Nonsense,' Archer snorted. 'I'm happy to help in my small way. It's rather exciting.'

Oliver had caught sight of his own reflection. 'I look like my father,' he said, his tone faintly horrified. 'And I'm due in court tomorrow morning. Please tell me this glue is easy to dissolve.'

Harry was almost tempted to test her disguise immediately, by wearing it to leave the theatre and stroll along the city streets; there was a freedom to dressing as a man that she'd found curiously enjoyable in the past. But that would mean passing the stage door manager, who would notice her changed appearance and could not be relied upon to stay silent. With some reluctance, she removed all traces of Mr Thompson and packed him neatly into the carpet bag provided by John Archer, alongside Oliver's disguise. They parted company with Archer outside the Garston Club with promises to visit him and his uncle at Thrumwell Manor in the near future.

'It's certainly been a busy evening,' Oliver said as they made their way towards Leicester Square. He gave Harry a sidelong look. 'Have you given any thought to how you're going to persuade the police to allow you – *us* – into their crime scene?'

She hesitated, aware that she was testing the boundaries of his good nature by asking him to use his professional connections to get access to the house on Berkeley Square. Yet what other option was available? She couldn't very well walk up to the front door and demand to be let in, the way Holmes might. 'I rather thought you might be able to help with that,' she said. 'You did say the police are at something of a loss.'

'I did and they are,' Oliver agreed. 'But I'm not sure they're desperate enough to call in Messrs Thompson and Gill – two mysterious strangers without an investigative qualification between them.'

It was an excellent point. Holmes had his reputation to fall back on, not to mention the grudging respect of several senior police officers. 'But they will be vouched for by the extremely well-regarded lawyer, Oliver Fortescue.' She summoned up a winning smile. 'I'm sure that will count for much.'

'I'm not a magician, Harry,' he grumbled, then sighed. 'But as it happens, there is someone I could ask. Someone who should appreciate the nuances of the situation, if not the particulars.'

Harry glanced at him, instantly intrigued. 'Oh? Whatever do you mean?'

But Oliver refused to be drawn. 'It's going to need delicate handling. Leave it with me.'

His expression was set and Harry knew better than to push

for more. He hadn't let her down yet. 'Thank you. Between this, and Polly, and Serafina, I know I'm asking a lot.' She took a deep breath. 'I'll completely understand if you want to say no.'

He laughed. 'I'm not sure I could, even if I wanted to. You're a hard woman to refuse, especially when you have your mind set on something.'

Something in his tone sent a warm tingle down her spine, the suggestion of admiration pleased her more than she wanted to admit. She concentrated on navigating the other pedestrians, determined to keep her reaction business-like. 'Even so, you must tell me if I go too far. I don't want to cause you problems.'

'Looking into Miss Eccleston is a favour to your family, rather than you,' Oliver countered. 'The matter with Polly is merely tying up loose ends from Mildred Longstaff's case, who was a client and therefore still a matter of interest to me. So you're only making one request on your own behalf and I must confess to a certain amount of curiosity of my own with regard to that, in spite of the risks.'

'Really?' She eyed him with some surprise. He'd been so against the notion of investigating that she hadn't considered his own interest had been piqued.

'Really,' he said as they reached the entrance to the Underground. 'You'll make a Watson of me yet.'

Harry smiled. 'There's no one I'd rather have,' she said, and reached for the carpet bag. 'Goodnight, Mr Gill.'

Oliver inclined his head gravely. 'Goodnight, Mr Thompson. Or is it Miss Moss?'

'Just Harry to you,' she said, squeezing his arm before turning away to enter the station. 'Always just Harry.'

But as she made her way down to the platform, she was uncomfortably aware of the fluttering in her stomach, the glow in her cheeks that had nothing to do with the sudden warmth of the station air. The more time she spent with Oliver, the more she was reminded of all things about him she admired; his quick mind, dry wit and unerring determination to do what was right. Not to mention his good looks, courteous manners and excellent taste in wine. He really did make it difficult to keep a clear head, she thought with some exasperation. One thing was certain, she decided as the train approached. Sherlock Holmes had never had this problem.

5

As with many fashionable areas of London, the people on the streets before dawn each morning were very different to those seen once the sun had risen to a respectable height in the sky, and Berkeley Square was no exception to this. Harry had groaned when her alarm clock had dragged her from her dreams at five-thirty, but she had risen and dressed in scruffy trousers, a worn coat and a grubby flat cap pulled low over her eyes. Wearily, she slipped out into the shadows of Mayfair, just another labourer on his way to work. In the half-light, street cleaners whistled to each other as they gathered the rubbish that had accumulated overnight. A chimney sweep cradled his brooms with purpose as he crossed the road in front of her, nodding a greeting, and a baker's boy rang his bell to warn her of his approach, his cart loaded with deliveries. The Georgian terraced houses overlooking the square were dark and silent, save for the occasional light in the lower-floor windows as the domestic staff prepared the house to greet the day. Neither the sweep nor the baker's boy were destined for the immaculate front doors that faced Berkeley Square. They were aiming for the tradesman's entrance, which Harry imagined would be accessed by back alleys on each side of the square. She intended to satisfy herself on that point shortly, but not before she had taken a stroll past the house where the theft had taken place.

It was easily identified by the burly policeman standing guard at the front door. Harry took care not to seem too curious as she passed by, even though she longed to study the unlit windows to see if they might have offered a way inside. Apart from its lone sentry, she saw nothing to differentiate number 48 from the other houses in the row – they were all four storeys tall, white stucco walls with attic windows peeping from the roof tiles. She supposed it might be possible to scramble across the rooftops and enter through an open window but that possibility would have been one of the first things considered by Scotland Yard. Apart from the windows, there were no other obvious entry points, at least from the front. Satisfied there was nothing more to be gleaned, Harry made her way to the end of the square and set about finding the tradesman's entrance.

The alleyway lay on Charles Street, heralded by an archway wide enough to admit a cart and lit by an electric lantern hanging overhead. Harry slowed as she approached, wary that there might be a police guard here too, but there was no uniformed presence to deter her. She passed by once, as though on her way somewhere else, and glanced past the yellow circle of light and into the gloom beyond. As far as she could tell, the alleyway was empty. She kept walking, turning the corner into Hays Mews and pausing as though lost. In the unlikely event that someone was observing her, they would have seen a puzzled young man slap his forehead and turn on his heel to duck confidently into the alley.

She made her way along the lit passage, squinting into the

shadow that followed until it widened into a long, rectangular courtyard. One side was lined with doors that Harry assumed corresponded to the houses facing into Berkeley Square, and the other with properties on Hays Mews. Each door was lit by a small lamp fastened to the wall, spilling a meagre glow onto a brass plaque and a button to press for attention. She crept forward, glancing cautiously around to ensure no one watched from the darkened windows, and paused beside number 48. There did not seem to be anything unusual – no tell-tale scratches or marks on the fittings to suggest someone had picked the lock. Harry craned her head, peering up at the windows. A ladder might offer access to the upper floors, but it was hardly an inconspicuous approach and the household staff hadn't reported anything amiss. She took in the roof, once again observing that a sure-footed thief might find it possible to enter through an attic window, had one been left ajar. But this was not an opportunistic crime, she reminded herself; a window would need to be opened by arrangement, and the police seemed satisfied that none of the staff had been involved in the theft. Her gaze travelled thoughtfully down the walls and over those of the neighbouring houses. All seemed equally solid and impenetrable. How had the burglars got in and out without being seen?

A sharp rustling in the alleyway caused the hair on the back of Harry's neck to stand on end. She whirled around, staring into the darkness. Was it a policeman making his rounds? Had she been seen ducking into the passage? What could she say to explain her presence? She tensed, preparing herself to barge past the newcomer and flee to safety. And then a low growl snaked towards her, followed by a volley of high-pitched barks. Damn. That changed things. A dog might snap and bite, catching hold of her trousers or coat and delaying her escape.

And from the sound of things, it had already picked up her scent.

'Pipe down, Rosie,' a coarse male voice grumbled. 'It's too early for that racket.'

A moment later, the dog appeared in the courtyard, brown-and-white ears flattened against its wiry skull as it glared balefully at Harry. A low rumble continued to sound and she saw it was a terrier of some kind, scruffy and unbrushed and tethered by a length of string attached to a frayed collar. The string was held by a dirty, stoop-shouldered man, who also carried a number of narrow metal cages. Matted grey tufts sprouted from beneath a sagging cloth cap and a voluminous overcoat flapped around his body as he came to an abrupt halt. His gaze narrowed at the sight of Harry. 'What have we here, then? A thief come to steal old Welcome's earnings?'

The dog growled again and Harry decided she did not want to cross either of them. Shaking her head, she summoned up a rough Cockney accent. 'No, mister. I came for a job. Only there ain't no one answering.'

The man sniffed. 'Not surprised at this hour.' He eyed her with increased suspicion. 'What kind of job?'

'Errand boy,' Harry said, thinking fast. Her size might make her appear younger than she was, especially in the gloom. 'At number 50.'

The dog was still snarling with mistrust but broke off when the old man gave a sharp tug on the string. 'That's enough, I say.' He glared at Harry. 'Just you stay there while I check my traps. I'll soon know if you're lying.'

Harry could only stare at him. Traps? What on earth could he mean by that? And then her attention fell on the metal cages over one shoulder, and the presence of the terrier at his side, and she knew. 'You're a rat catcher.'

'The best there is,' he said, sounding proud. 'If you was from round here, you'd have heard the name Welcome Dobbs and no mistake.'

Without waiting for a response, he limped to a shadowy, unlit corner of the yard and knelt. Rosie seemed torn between continuing to glower at Harry and following her master, but after a moment she scampered towards the corner, ears pricking up as she went. There was a clang of metal, a yap from Rosie and a grunt from the old man. Harry did not want to imagine what the traps held but it seemed to satisfy the rat catcher. Getting to his feet, he turned to study Harry once more and she saw two limp bodies in his hands. She tried to look unperturbed as they were swiftly stowed into the tattered bag that crossed his body. 'You want to be careful of that house,' he rasped, nodding towards the door at Harry's shoulder. 'Got a bad history, it has.'

She risked a glance backwards. Which house did he mean? 'Number 50?'

Dobbs nodded. 'Oh, it looks nice enough from the outside but old Welcome don't go much on appearances.' He paused to toss something down to the dog, who snapped it up and settled on her scrawny haunches, watching him expectantly. 'Old Welcome sees beyond what's obvious.'

He gave Harry such a penetrating look that she was convinced that he saw straight through her carefully applied boot polish grime and too-big coat. She resisted the urge to pull her cap more firmly over her hair. But surely he meant number 48, where the robbery had taken place? 'I know there's a bobby on the door,' she ventured. 'That ain't good news for anyone.'

'Not that one.' Dobbs jerked his head sideways. 'The house next door. Been empty for more than ten years, and I ain't surprised after what happened there.'

Harry frowned. The house did not look empty. Curtains hung at the windows, the steps were scrubbed and the door looked as though it had recently been repainted. 'What did happen there?'

The old man shrugged. 'Terrible things. Murder.'

He laced the final word with the kind of dramatic, guttural dread that Harry imagined John Archer would give a great deal to be able to imitate. 'Murder?' she echoed. 'In a fancy place like this?'

'Evil ain't picky,' he said, and spat hard at the ground. 'It was years ago. They say a man went mad and murdered his woman, and her ghost haunts the house still. Anyone who spends the night there is driven mad with the terror of it.'

The story sent an uneasy shiver down Harry's spine. She squared her shoulders. 'I don't believe in ghosts.'

'That's what the others said,' Dobbs replied, and his grin revealed several missing teeth. 'All I know is no one has stayed there more than a few nights in all the years I've been catching round here, saving them what's in there now. It does my business no harm to have an empty house. More rats then. More money from the neighbouring gaffs who want 'em caught.'

She did her best not to shudder. 'But it's not empty now.'

'No,' he conceded. 'More's the pity. But they won't stay. It's a shame after they spent all that money tarting it up. Even filled in the old coiners' tunnel, so I heard.'

Harry blinked. Coiners was a term she'd come across in a number of Holmes' adventures. It was slang for the criminal gangs who specialised in forging money, particularly coins. In real life, they had been rife before the turn of the century but several high-profile captures had seen the counterfeiters turn their attentions to other crimes. 'Did you say tunnel?' she asked Dobbs.

'I did, leading right underneath this courtyard and coming out a full street away.' He grinned. 'Full of rats, it was. A tidy income for old Welcome, 'til they closed it up.'

'Interesting,' Harry breathed. She glanced up at the house. 'You know what, I don't fancy working there now. Not after hearing all that.'

Welcome Dobbs nodded approvingly. 'You do right, lad.' He tossed Rosie another titbit and sniffed. 'Try Hamilton Square. You might get lucky if you mention my name.'

She smiled, because the advice was kindly given. 'Ta very much. I – er – hope your traps are full, Mr Dobbs.'

He sighed as he turned towards the alley that led out of the yard. 'Not as full as they used to be. Come on, Rosie. Let's see what we can get for these wretches.'

Harry waited a full five minutes before she followed, gazing thoughtfully back and forth between number 48 and 50 and considering everything she had learned. She doubted the tall tales of murder and hauntings had any bearing on the theft of the Sora-Sora diamond but the fact that the property had been used by criminals in the past was definitely a point of curiosity. The coiners described by Sir Arthur Conan Doyle had been desperate, ruthless men and Harry had no doubt their real-life counterparts had been the same. Could the tunnel Dobbs mentioned have some connection to this new crime? It certainly seemed plausible, Harry mused as she made her way home to start her day all over again. In fact, it was just possible she had uncovered a significant clue.

* * *

It was by no means certain that Beth would receive Harry's letter in time to meet her at twelve-thirty, but she set out for

Regent's Park all the same. Nor had she settled on the best way to approach the matter of infiltrating the Hot Spot with Seb. Her note had been brief, simply asking Beth to meet her beside the fountain in St John's Lodge Gardens that afternoon, but Harry had spent much of the morning wrestling with the conundrum of how much she should confide in the young woman. Beth had proved trustworthy so far, but she knew nothing of Harry's true identity. Introducing her to Seb would open a door that could never be closed again. And yet Harry couldn't see a way round it: she needed Beth to be her eyes and ears inside the Hot Spot, to see what she could uncover. She had managed to persuade her brother to arrange entry to the club that evening, shamelessly dropping into the conversation that it had been Oliver's idea that he accompany her. But she had not managed to convince him that, once inside, she would seek out Serafina on her own.

'Absolutely not, Harry,' he'd said when she had called him the night before, and the words had rung with unaccustomed steel. 'I'll get you in, but you stay with me for the duration of the evening and you leave by midnight. Lawrence will have my hide otherwise.'

'But how am I supposed to find out what Serafina wants?' Harry objected. 'Everyone knows who you are – she probably knows you, at least by reputation, and even if she doesn't, someone will tell her.'

Seb sighed. 'I'm not sure what you expect me to do about that. Pretend to be someone else?'

It was a possibility that had occurred to her already, until she remembered how terrible Seb had been at amateur dramatics in their younger years. 'Of course not, you're far too easily recognisable.' She paused. 'But I'm not.'

He laughed. 'I hate to break it to you, Sis, but the Hot Spot is – well – hot. Meaning the place will be teeming with people you know – the Goldsworthy sisters, the Chartwells and plenty more, as well as those who know you by reputation. If you're hoping for an incognito meeting with Miss Eccleston then I'm afraid you're going to be disappointed.'

Harry hesitated, toying with the telephone cable, but she could not bring herself to suggest she wore a disguise. 'I don't know how I'm supposed to find out anything.'

'Talk to people,' Seb suggested. 'Lips get surprisingly loose as the night wears on. And if nothing else, you'll have some fun.' He stopped as though reviewing his own words. 'A very little fun.'

'I might want to bring a friend,' Harry said, giving in to the inevitable.

'The more the merrier,' her brother replied. 'Anyone I know? It's not Fortescue, is it?'

'No,' Harry said quickly.

'No, I suppose that really wouldn't do, would it?' Seb mused. 'All right, I'll need your friend's name by tea-time tomorrow to arrange the invitations. What do you want to drink?'

Harry thought back to the newspaper reports she'd read about the over-inflated prices charged by nightclubs and tried not to wince. 'Whatever you're having.'

'Champagne it is,' Seb said. 'Don't forget to call me with the name.'

Which had left Harry wondering how Beth would react to the suggestion that she join them at the Hot Spot. A small part of her hoped the other woman hadn't received her letter in time; if she didn't appear then Harry could spend a pleasant half-hour walking among the hidden passages between the winter foliage and then return to her office without having to risk her identity. But that hope was quashed when she reached the fountain and saw Beth waiting. Squaring her shoulders, Harry approached, waiting for the light of recognition to dawn on the other woman's face. It did not take long.

'Blimey, you scrub up well.' Beth's gaze was narrow as she took in Harry's expensive shoes, fitted woollen coat and fashionable hat, in sharp contrast to her own clean but well-worn clothes. 'You'll be telling me next your name ain't Sarah Smith.'

'I think you already knew that.' She held out a hand. 'Harry White.'

Beth's nose wrinkled. 'Is that another made-up name? 'Cos you don't talk like any of the Harrys I know.'

'It's short for Harriet,' Harry said, smiling. 'And I'm sorry I pretended to be someone else. It was necessary at the time.'

'When you was nosing around Mrs Haverford's Bureau of Excellence, you mean?' Beth nodded. 'I don't think you'd have got through the door if you'd gone as yourself.'

Harry took a breath. 'Exactly.' She glanced around, making sure no one was within earshot, but the day was dull and grey and threatening sleet. They had the garden to themselves. 'Shall we walk a little? There are quite a few things I need to explain and I don't have very much time.'

To her credit, Beth did not interrupt as Harry laid out the reasons she had adopted the alias of Sarah Smith, nor did she raise an eyebrow when Harry explained in more detail the reason for her interest in Serafina Eccleston. She listened to everything, an inscrutable expression on her face, and continued to walk in silence for almost a minute once Harry finished speaking.

'I wondered why you was interested in a dance hostess,' she said eventually. 'Thought maybe she was in the family way, like your friend in Brighton.'

Harry blanched. She meant Cecily Earnshaw, a young

woman whom Simeon Pemberton had seduced and abandoned when she became pregnant, but the idea that there might be a time-pressing reason for Rufus to marry Serafina had not occurred to Harry. 'I hope not.'

'That'd put the cat among the canaries, wouldn't it?' Beth flashed a brief, humourless smile. 'But it ain't smart, not if she's got the kind of ambitions you say. You get the ring first, see?'

Harry did see. Men had been denying responsibility for pregnancies outside of wedlock since the concept of marriage had first been invented. If Serafina really was a gold digger, she'd want to be assured of her reward before she took such a risk. 'But what if she's not ambitious? What if she loves him?'

Beth shrugged. 'You won't know until you meet her. And even then you might not be able to tell – not if she's good. I knew a girl who's as common as a crow, spent a bit of money on learning to talk nice and read a few books on manners. Now she's married to some posh bloke and living in a big house and no one has any idea what a grubby-kneed kid she used to be.'

It was her mother's worst fear, Harry thought gloomily, and sighed. 'Rufus certainly seems to be smitten.'

'I expect he is,' Beth said evenly. 'And maybe she's sweet on him in return. But I'll tell you something I bet he don't know. Her name ain't Serafina.'

Harry stopped walking. 'How do you know that?'

Beth looked pleased with herself. 'I chatted up one of the Hot Spot bottle boys,' she replied, then caught sight of Harry's puzzled expression. 'The ones what clear out the empties each morning. Anyway, he'd never heard of her, but he asked the kid he was working with and he said, "Oh, you mean Ida. She works the late shift, Thursdays to Sundays."'

The simplicity of Beth's approach impressed Harry. Why

hadn't she thought of doing something like that? 'Did you find out anything else?'

'Not much,' Beth admitted. 'I told them I was looking for work and I'd been given Serafina's name by a mutual friend. And here's the interesting bit. The one who called her Ida said I shouldn't hang about, on account of her not working there for much longer.'

Harry digested this. It certainly seemed to dovetail with the couple's plan to elope. 'Did he say why?'

'He said she was due an inheritance,' Beth answered. 'But he sort of smirked when he said it, and tapped his nose as if it wasn't really an inheritance at all.'

Not an inheritance, perhaps, but an allowance, Harry thought, alongside an expectation that anyone who married into the wealthy Abinger family need not trouble themselves with work. 'Ida isn't quite as glamorous as Serafina, is it?' she said, making a mental note to pass this fresh information on to Oliver as soon as she could.

Beth snorted. 'Serafina sounds like the kind of woman who spends all day floating around a butterfly house. I prefer Ida.'

But another thought had occurred to Harry. 'Do you think either of the bottle boys would recognise you?'

She shook her head. 'Nah. They don't start work until the morning, so they never mix with the toffs.'

'Very well,' Harry said, taking the assurance at face value. 'If my brother is to be believed, there will be several other guests who know me, which will make it impossible for me to be much more than a distraction while you do the real digging.'

Beth regarded her steadily. 'There's just one problem with that. I ain't got nothing to wear.'

It was an objection Harry had been expecting. Beth was taller than her, and her feet looked to be at least one size bigger.

She was broader across the shoulders too, meaning there was nothing in Harry's own wardrobe that would hang well on her. She dug into her handbag for the money she'd added that morning. 'Use this,' she said, offering it to Beth. 'You'll need a dress, some shoes and a coat. I can lend you a handbag and some jewellery.'

The other woman did not take the notes. 'I don't need charity.'

'But you do need to look the part and that costs money,' Harry replied, with gentle but firm insistence. 'Think of it as necessary expenses, no different to me paying for your train tickets when you were investigating Polly.'

This justification seemed to do the trick. The money disappeared into Beth's pocket. 'I don't know what my old mum's going to think when she sees me dressed up all fancy.'

Harry took a deep breath. 'I thought about that. Would you prefer to change into your new clothes at my place?'

'Your place?' A frown creased Beth's brow as she considered the offer. 'I suppose it depends on where it is.'

'Mayfair,' Harry said. 'Hamilton Square.'

Beth quirked her lips. 'Very nice. Won't your butler notice?'

'I don't have one,' Harry said, and felt a pang of reproach at the thought of Chesterton, the Abinger family butler. 'At least, not in London. I live alone, as it happens, in a small apartment that suits me perfectly.'

'Good for you,' she said, favouring Harry with a considering gaze. 'In that case, I accept.'

Reaching into her purse again, Harry withdrew a small rectangle of card, upon which she had written her address. 'I will be home at five o'clock, if that suits you.'

'It does,' Beth said, taking the card and tucking it away.

'Excellent,' Harry replied. 'Which brings me to my final

question. My brother needs to supply our names in advance of our visit. What do you want to be called?'

The question gave Beth a moment's pause. 'Lizzie,' she said at length. 'Lizzie Devine. That's posh enough, I reckon.'

Harry turned it over in her mind, making sure Beth hadn't accidentally hit upon the name of someone she already knew. 'Perfect,' she said. 'Enjoy your shopping trip. You should find everything you need in Selfridges.'

The other woman grinned. 'Selfridges? No fear. I'm off to Petticoat Lane, thank you very much.'

The market that crowded the length of Middlesex Street was still called Petticoat Lane, in spite of the road being renamed more than a century earlier. It was as famous for its silver-tongued street traders as it was for the dubious goods they sold but Harry suspected Beth was too shrewd to be taken in by smooth sales talk. Shopping there might even mean some money left over from the crisp notes she had handed over. Not that she begrudged the expense, which was entirely necessary to find out the truth about Serafina – or Ida – Eccleston.

'As long as you're able to get everything you need, I don't mind where you go,' Harry replied. 'I'll see you later. We can plan everything in more detail then.'

'See you later,' Beth echoed, and cocked her head. 'It's nice to meet you properly, Harry White. I think we're going to have some fun together.'

6

Harry wasn't sure what she'd been expecting the entrance of the Hot Spot to look like, but she had not imagined a shabby black front door that simply bore a brass knocker and no number.

'That's rather the point,' Seb murmured when she expressed her surprise as they climbed out of the cab. 'It's a private party, only accessible by invitation. It's supposed to be nondescript, at least on the outside.'

He gave one short rap on the door knocker and stood back expectantly. Beside him, Beth merely shrugged, as though she attended illicit bottle parties in Soho every night of the week. She certainly looked the part, Harry thought, feeling alarmingly drab in comparison. Her dress was long, a flash of azure-blue satin peeping from beneath the sumptuous, almost floor-length coat wrapped over the top. She had not seemed the least disappointed when Harry confessed she did not own a fur stole to complete the look. Her dark hair was fastened into a sleek bun at the nape of her neck, coaxed into fashionable waves that framed her neat features and transformed her into an elegant reinvention of a bright young thing, the thrilling group who had ruled London's nightclub scene for most of the previous decade. And she had managed to buy everything she needed at a fraction of the money it would have cost at Selfridges.

'I drive a hard bargain,' she'd explained over tea in Harry's apartment, when Harry had exclaimed over the amount she'd tried to return to her.

'Then you earned it,' Harry said, shaking her head in astonishment. 'Consider whatever is left as payment for this evening.'

Seb was quite taken with her too, beaming with approval when Harry introduced him to her friend Lizzie in the taxi cab. 'What an utter delight to meet you, Miss Devine. I can tell you are exactly the kind of friend my sister needs to rescue her from self-imposed spinsterhood.'

Beth smiled, her cheeks dimpling as she dipped her head. 'Charmed, I'm sure.'

Deciding as they dressed that it would be too risky for Beth to attempt to disguise her Cockney accent, they had invented a wealthy merchant father who indulged his daughter's ambitions of rising above her East End roots. They kept the details of how and where the two of them had met vague – at some get-together or another would suffice – and agreed that admitting to a loose connection would allow Beth to drift away as the night wore on, the better to undertake her mission. Thankfully, it appeared Seb was too captivated by Beth's appearance to question the likelihood of his sister making such an acquaintance.

Gerrard Street was in the heart of Soho, an area of such wild reputation that Harry had not felt the need to visit. She took the opportunity to gaze curiously around as they waited for the door to be opened, taking in the crowd spilling from the pub on one corner and resisting the temptation to tap her foot to the music floating above the laughter and chatter on the frosty air. It was not yet ten o'clock, perhaps too early for the wildest behaviour to manifest itself, but she could only see people enjoying themselves. It seemed to her that rumours of Soho's debauchery were greatly exaggerated.

'Ah,' Seb said, turning an expectant look towards the door at the sound of bolts being drawn back. 'Open sesame.'

The door was pulled back enough for a sharp-faced, diminutive woman to peer out at them. She looked them up and down in turn, showing no sign of recognition as her scowl travelled over Seb. He smiled in return. 'How are you this evening, Nell? You look as radiant as ever.'

The woman was unmoved by his honeyed tone. 'Names?' she snapped.

Seb remained unperturbed. 'Samuel Black, Hortensia Croft and the esteemed Laura Doone.'

Harry did not dare glance at Beth as he pronounced the unfamiliar names. Nell made a show of consulting a dog-eared notebook, somehow managing to eye them with disfavour at the same time. After a moment, she let out a grunt of satisfaction and opened the door wide enough to allow them inside, slamming the bolts home as though shutting out a pack of crazed wolves. The hallway beyond the door was narrow and badly lit. One yellowed bulb hung from the ceiling, revealing peeling wallpaper and a threadbare carpet that led to a single staircase at the far end. It was not the most welcoming of entrances and Harry could only hope the club beyond was better furnished.

'Sign here,' Nell demanded, pointing to another book, this one on a small table behind the door. Seb bent to scribble carelessly on the page, then handed the pen to Harry. She squinted down at the writing, locating the name Seb had given for her and saw that the neighbouring column detailed an order for a bottle of champagne. Trying to look natural, she jiggled the pen to create a perfectly illegible signature. Beth followed suit and placed the pen on the paper. Beside them, Seb peeled off three pound notes and handed them to Nell, who took them without smiling.

'Up the stairs,' Nell said, jerking her head towards the end of the hallway. 'Ask for Albert.'

Seb made a little bow. 'Always a pleasure, Nell.'

Harry thought she saw a faint softening around the woman's eyes. 'Don't know what you mean, Mr Black. We never met before tonight.'

Harry waited until they had reached the bottom of the rickety staircase before turning to her brother. 'Hortensia Croft?'

He gave a sage nod. 'First rule of bottle parties, Sis. Never give your real name on the paperwork.'

She saw Beth suppress a smile. 'I'll be sure to remember that.'

The door at the top of the stairs was every bit as nondescript as the one facing the street. Seb rapped on it with his knuckles and they waited again, although Harry could now feel the vibration of an insistent beat through the barely covered floorboards. After the scrape of more bolts being drawn back, this door opened to reveal a heavy gorilla of a man who stared out at them without any discernible expression. 'Yeah?'

'Hello, Pierre,' Seb replied pleasantly, raising his voice to be heard over the music that was now thumping from beyond the man. 'We're here to see Albert.'

'Names?'

With a patience that was evidently born of experience, Seb

repeated the false names he had given Nell at the front door. Pierre ran a thick finger down the list he held and nodded. 'Welcome to the Hot Spot. Albert will be delighted you're joining him this evening.'

They stepped past him into another corridor, much shorter than the entrance hall below. This one also ended in a door, but it was swept open as they approached. A blast of frantic jazz hit them, the wail of trumpets mingling with the heavy thud of the beat and sibilant hiss of the brush on snare. Accompanying it was a torrid swirl of heat, the foetid air laced with a heady haze of smoke and alcohol fumes that swarmed over them with the fury of a sandstorm. But it was the scene expanding before them that really took Harry's breath away. What looked like the entire upper floor had been opened into one enormous room. The band occupied a small raised dais along the furthest wall, with a dance floor in front that was filled with moving bodies. White-clothed tables were dotted at regular intervals, surrounded by chairs. Elsewhere, Harry saw armchairs and settees, grouped around low tables. All were lit by crimson-shaded lamps that painted everything a deep, unsettling red. It put Harry in mind of Dante's *Inferno*, which described a journey through Hell. She shook the thought away. Really, what had she expected?

As they reached the threshold, a dark-haired man dressed in an immaculate cream suit stepped into their path, his arms thrown wide in exuberant welcome. 'Mr Black, it is so good to see you!'

Seb's mouth quirked. 'Albert, I presume?'

'The very same!' the man cried, his luxurious black moustache quivering as he waved them through the door. 'It's an honour to welcome you to my humble abode.'

Harry heard Beth snort. 'If this is his home, I'm the Queen of Sheba.'

Albert turned his smile upon her and widened it to include Harry. 'But where are my manners? Which of you is Miss Croft and which is Miss Doone?'

Beth surprised Harry by stepping forward, her hand outstretched. 'Lizzie Devine. Pleased to make your acquaintance.'

Albert let out a gurgle of delight as he took her hand. 'The pleasure is all mine, I assure you.' He eyed Harry with undisguised amusement, giving her the distinct impression he knew not only her real name, but her relationship to Seb too. 'And what may I call you this evening, dear lady?'

She sighed. 'Would you believe me if I said Hortensia?'

His laughter was a shout. 'Here you can be whomever you choose and someone entirely different tomorrow.' He leaned towards her confidingly. 'Tonight, we shall be Albert and Hortensia, yet with the dawn, we may shake off those names like serpents shedding their skins.'

Harry blinked. 'Well… quite.'

And then Seb was there, tucking her hand under his arm. 'Will you show us to our table? I suspect darling Hortensia is in need of a drink. The heat, you understand.'

'Of course,' Albert said, with a small bow.

Harry caught any number of interested looks being cast their way as they wove between the tables to a comfortable velvet banquette curved around a table at the back of the room. It offered a clear view of the band, the dance floor and many of the other guests, and was clearly a premium seat, reserved for the very best customers. That, together with the easy familiarity with which Seb had navigated the hurdles to get inside, told

Harry that this was not his first visit to the Hot Spot. Given the dangers Oliver had hinted lay within its walls, she wasn't sure how she felt about that. But there was no doubt that his acquaintance with the club had benefitted her this evening. Perhaps it was best not to dwell too much on what Seb might have got up to in the past, especially since it was the actions of Rufus that had launched the family crisis they were trying to defuse.

Albert waved an expansive arm. 'Please, make yourselves comfortable. *Mi casa es su casa.*'

'My house is your house,' Harry murmured to Beth, seeing her brow furrow ever so slightly.

Taking their coats, their host gave another ingratiating bow. 'Your drinks will arrive momentarily.'

Harry slid behind the table and took the opportunity to examine their surroundings in more detail. Her first observation was that she was overdressed – not in terms of finery but definitely in terms of coverage. Many of the women she saw around her had bare shoulders and wore scandalously low necklines, while hemlines varied from floor-length to almost non-existent. The men, by contrast, wore dinner dress, although those on the dance floor had discarded their jackets and waistcoats. Some of the shirts had come untucked as they danced and others had dispensed with their collars. It was all so wonderfully unbuttoned and free.

'Did you spot Maud and Rosalind Goldsworthy as we came in?' Seb asked. 'They certainly saw you so we shall have to say hello at some point.'

Harry's gaze swept across the tables until she saw the two sisters, holding court among a small group of other young men and women. 'Isn't that Cecil Porter with them?'

Her brother nodded. 'And Josephine Dibley. She's the star

of Noël Coward's new play. Beside her is Ivor Novello – another of Noël's darlings.'

'Is there anyone here you don't know?' she asked.

Seb laughed. 'Of course. I'm sure you'll have realised this isn't my first visit to the Hot Spot but I'm not a regular. Which is why our little brother's attachment to Miss Eccleston escaped my notice.'

The mention of the name caused Harry to glance across the room once more, this time seeking out those who might be working as dance hostesses. She saw white-coated waiters carrying trays of drinks, others attending to champagne buckets, but there were no women waiting on the tables. Frowning, she turned back to Seb and beckoned Beth nearer. 'How are we to discover which one is Serafina?'

'I imagine the hostess assigned to us will make herself known once the drinks arrive,' he said. 'We could always ask her.'

Harry exchanged a look with Beth. 'We don't want to raise any suspicions,' she said. 'Let's give it half an hour, then Lizzie here can slip away and make some discreet enquiries.'

Seb glanced back and forth between them. 'Why do I get the feeling I'm surplus to requirements here?'

'Nonsense,' Harry said, patting his arm. 'You're our secret weapon. Tell me what goes on here on a typical night.'

His expression grew slightly wary. 'What do you mean?'

She fought the temptation to roll her eyes. Really, did he still consider her so very unworldly? 'I read the newspapers, Seb, I'm well aware we're in a den of iniquity.' She laced the final three words with unmistakable sarcasm. 'But it might be helpful to get an idea of the extent of the place. I don't see any card games, for example – is there a separate room for gamblers?'

'Yes,' he replied, and she sensed his reluctance to elaborate. 'There's a card room on the top floor, along with some private chambers for more intimate encounters.'

Harry was determined not to blush. 'Do you mean there's a brothel?'

He raised an eyebrow. 'No, that's two doors down. These rooms are for consenting guests who want to get to know each other better. Much better. Usually in a group.'

'Oh.' Harry sat back against the velvet seat, feeling her cheeks turn scarlet. 'How... Bohemian.'

She was saved from her brother's knowing grin by the arrival of a waiter bearing a silver champagne bucket, followed by another expertly balancing a tray laden with three crystal flutes on the splayed fingertips of one hand. The glasses were deposited on the table in deferential silence, then the champagne cork was popped. Harry felt Beth quivering beside her, despite the other woman's outwardly cool expression, and realised it must be the first time she had ever seen it done. 'Small sips,' she whispered, as the waiter filled the flutes with golden, fizzing bubbles. 'It looks harmless but it's lethal if you drink it too fast.'

Beth gave her a look that reminded Harry she had watched her put away several pints of mild and be seemingly none the worse for wear. But they needed clear heads for what they were about to do. The appearance of drunkenness was desirable. Actual drunkenness was not. 'Spoilsport,' Beth grumbled, taking the flute Seb was offering her. 'Whenever else am I going to get a bottle of the good stuff?'

Taking a miniscule sip from her own glass, Harry allowed herself a moment to savour the burst of buttery richness on her tongue before resuming her study of the clientele. As she got used to the movement between tables, the ebb and flow of friends as they mingled and greeted one another, she began to pick out subtle differences in demeanour among some of the women she observed. While appearing to laugh and enjoy the company of the table where they sat, there was a watchfulness behind their merriment, as though they were not truly part of the group, despite draping themselves across the men in a manner that was decidedly over-familiar. She didn't observe many of them dancing; in fact, they seemed more concerned with topping up glasses that were not empty.

'They work on commission,' Seb said, noticing her narrowed gaze. 'The more people drink, the more they earn. And speaking of which...'

Looking up, Harry saw a young woman in a skimpy sequinned dress sashaying towards them, a glossy black bob swishing as she moved and a wide smile on her expertly made-up face. 'Our hostess, I presume.'

She reached them before Seb could confirm Harry's assertion. 'Now this looks like my kind of table,' she said, with a broad wink. Her accent was considerably more refined than Beth's but left Harry in no doubt that she was London born and bred. Shrewd blue eyes travelled over each of them in swift assessment, before coming to rest on Seb. 'Mind if I join you?'

He patted the velvet in clear invitation. 'I'd be utterly thrilled if you would.'

Smiling, she slid in beside him and placed an empty glass on the table. 'Allow me,' Seb said, reaching for the champagne and filling the flute to the brim. 'I'm Samuel, this is Hortensia and her friend, Lizzie.'

'Louisa,' she said, and eyed Harry with some sympathy. 'That's quite a name you've got there. Do you often get mistaken for someone's maiden aunt?'

'It is a heavy burden,' Harry said, sighing as though acknowledging a lifelong curse. 'I can't even shorten it.'

'Not like Sam and Liz, here,' Louisa smiled as she batted Seb playfully on the arm. 'You can call me Lou, if you like. Now that we're friends.'

There was nothing subtle about her approach, Harry observed in wry amusement, but it seemed the Hot Spot was not a place for subtlety. From the lighting to the décor to the fast-paced jazz thrumming on the air, everything screamed excess. And it must work; the place was almost full and it wasn't even eleven o'clock.

Seb was clearly content to play the part of a man eager for attention. 'I do so enjoy making new friends,' he said, clinking his glass against Louisa's with a conspiratorial smile.

At the furthest end of the table, Beth put a hand to her cheek and sighed loudly. 'I do believe that champagne has gone right to my head. I might just go and freshen up.' She rose, which caused Seb to stand too, and made her way around the edge of the table. 'I won't be long.'

Harry watched her leave, trying not to wonder just how she might go about finding Serafina. Idly, she sipped her champagne, listening to Louisa's too-bright chatter and watching the dancers move to the swinging beat. She spotted Albert weaving between tables, pausing here and there to offer a solicitous greeting. Maud Goldsworthy had climbed on top of the table she shared with her group and seemed to be reciting poetry, although it could have been her cook's shopping list for all Harry knew. And then her gaze came to rest upon a face she knew well. Percy Finchem was seated on the periphery of the Goldsworthys and he was gazing straight back at her. He raised a hand in greeting.

Stifling a groan, Harry turned to her brother. 'Percy Finchem is here.'

Seb nodded. 'Oh, yes, I saw him as we came in.' A wicked smile tugged at his mouth. 'Perhaps it's your lucky night.'

'Ha ha,' she replied, reaching for her glass. It didn't matter that Percy was here, she told herself. Perhaps he would be content with a friendly wave across the room. Perhaps she wouldn't have to contend with the smile that did odd things to her innards.

'Don't look now but he's coming over,' Seb remarked.

Glancing up through her lashes, Harry saw that he was right. Percy was threading his way through the tables, making a beeline for them. She fired a meaningful glare at Seb. 'Do not encourage him.'

Her brother smirked. 'From what I've seen, he doesn't need any encouragement.'

Before she could respond, a shadow fell across the table. 'Miss White. What an unexpected joy to find you here.'

Composing herself, Harry looked up with a polite smile. 'Hello, Percy. How are you?'

Seb stood, extending a hand. 'Good to see you, Finchem.'

'And you,' Percy replied. 'In the company of the ever-lovely Louisa, too.'

The other woman smiled but it did not quite reach her eyes. 'Thank you, Mr Finchem.'

Harry felt her interest pique. Was it her imagination or was Louisa's manner suddenly a little stilted? But Percy was speaking again and this time he was addressing her. 'No Fortescue this evening?' he enquired, his tone studiously innocent.

'No.' Harry forced her own voice to match his lightness. 'He's not much of a dancer.'

Percy's eyes glittered. 'Happily for me.'

A treacherous bubble of pleasure burst somewhere in Harry's midriff, even as she offered a silent apology to Oliver for maligning his ability to dance. She tamped both emotions down, determined not to let Percy's outrageous flirtation affect her. But Seb had other ideas. 'Won't you join us for a drink?' he said, waving a careless hand at the champagne bottle. 'I'm sure Louisa can rustle up another glass from somewhere.'

Again, Harry caught a flicker of something else behind Louisa's smile. 'Of course I can.' She reached out to stroke Seb's cheek. 'Anything for you, Sam.'

Percy watched her leave, then eased along the banquette until he sat beside Harry. 'Sam, is it?'

Seb leaned back, the picture of relaxed unconcern. 'You know how it is. Who are you this evening?'

'I've never been one for pretending to be someone else,' Percy said, and his gaze flicked to Harry. 'What you see is what you get with me. As Miss White knows.'

That caused Seb's eyebrows to lift. 'Does she indeed?'

He shrugged. 'I've never hidden my interest in getting to know her better. Perhaps tonight is my chance.'

Seb snorted. 'I assume your brother isn't here.'

'No, he's away on family business,' Percy said, and turned the full force of his regard onto Harry. 'No James. No Fortescue. Just us, and an endless supply of champagne.'

For a moment, Harry was mesmerised by the blueness of his eyes. 'Surely not endless,' she said, breaking the spell just as Louisa materialised with another flute.

'Enough to make us dance, then,' Percy said. 'Please tell me you dance, Miss White.'

She glanced across the room to where some of the crowd had begun throwing themselves around with blissful disregard for propriety. 'If that's what you mean then I'm not sure I know how.'

He smiled. 'Luckily, I'm an excellent teacher.'

'You know, I feel like the perfect gooseberry,' Seb said mildly, handing Percy the filled flute. 'Do you mean to seduce my sister right before my eyes, Finchem?'

Percy's smile widened, and Harry was reminded of the way he had looked as they'd stood alone in the moonlight after a dinner party at Abinger Hall the previous November, wolfish and wild, with just a hint of wickedness. 'Only if she'll let me.'

The moment was broken by a sudden squeal from Louisa, who had knocked her glass sideways, sending a tide of golden liquid cascading across the tablecloth. 'Silly me,' she exclaimed, her face twisted in consternation.

Seemingly from nowhere, Albert appeared. He took in the spill and threw Seb an apologetic look. 'Accidents will happen,' he said, sighing. 'Please excuse us for a short while, to allow us to make things right.'

Obediently, the four of them slipped out from behind the table. Albert snapped his fingers at a passing waiter, who whisked the stained cloth away. 'Won't you join me at my table, Miss White?' Percy asked, placing a hand on the small of her back. 'I'm sure Sam here won't mind.'

Seb cast an enquiring look at Harry. It was a tempting offer; on another occasion she might have given in to the curiosity Percy aroused in her, but she wasn't at the Hot Spot to enjoy herself. With regret, she gave a barely perceptible shake of her head. 'I'm sorry, Finchem, but I do mind,' Seb replied blandly. 'Who knows what dark deeds you're getting up to over there.'

If Percy was put out, he didn't show it. 'Perhaps later,' he said, and gave Harry a look that left her in no doubt that he would make good on the suggestion. With a nod, he turned and made his way back through the tables, just as the waiter returned with a fresh tablecloth. Once it was smoothed into place, Albert ushered them back into their seats but before Harry could move, she realised Louisa was beside her. 'Watch yourself with that one,' the other woman breathed in her ear. 'He's not what he seems.'

Startled, Harry turned to stare at her, but Louisa's face was all smiles as she waved her forward. 'After you, Hortensia.'

Harry retook her seat, watching as Louisa slid next to Seb once more, beaming as though she did not have a care in the world. Had her warning been about Percy, Harry wondered? But of course it had – who else could she have been referring to? It echoed something Oliver had once said, along such similar lines that it might almost have been the exact same sentence. But what had prompted Louisa to offer such a warning, and to a virtual stranger? What might she know that Harry did not? More importantly, what did Oliver know?

'Let me top up your glass,' Seb said, reaching for Louisa's empty flute. 'You'd barely sipped from the last one.'

Louisa's giggling protests washed over Harry as she scanned the crowd, searching for Beth. She couldn't allow Louisa's whispered warning to distract her. With luck, Beth might have found Serafina, or at least be on her trail, and they would be one step closer to uncovering the truth about her attachment to Rufus. She ought to wait for Beth to return but she was suddenly overcome by a wave of impatience.

'Will you excuse me?' she said brightly, turning to Seb and Louisa. 'I think I see Lizzie waving over there.'

Her brother got to his feet. 'Of course.'

She felt Louisa's dark-eyed gaze following her as she left the table and wondered whether she suspected Harry might be going in search of Percy. Purposefully, she took a route that gave his table a wide berth, although she did pause to greet a number of other acquaintances as she made her way across the room. It was only when she had circumvented the dance floor and reached the far side that she was forced to concede she had no idea where Beth was. She'd been hoping to locate her as she walked but there had been no sign of her. What was more, she couldn't see a sign for the ladies' room, where she might at least gather her thoughts away from the heat and smoke and relentless thump of the music. Glancing around, she caught sight of a pair of doors in one corner. Like all the others she had seen since arriving outside, these were unmarked and offered no clue to what lay beyond them, but she couldn't see any other possibilities and her head was starting to ache. Grateful that they appeared to be unguarded, at least for the moment, she pushed against the wood and was relieved to discover they were not locked. A moment later, she was in another corridor, although this one was not quite as drab and threadbare as the one downstairs. The doors closed behind her, cutting off the trumpets. There were no scarlet lampshades here – the bulb over her head gave off a feeble yellow glow, creating puddles of shadow where the light did not reach. The air was not cool, but it was fresher than inside the club, and she was alone. Taking a deep breath, she hurried forward. The hallway split, one strand leading to a staircase, the other winding past into murky gloom, ending in what looked like another door. Recalling Seb's description of the chambers upstairs, Harry made for the door. To her relief, it led to a bathroom, one with a single cubicle and a cracked sink below a tarnished mirror. It did not appear to be meant for the use of guests but Harry did not care. She turned the cold tap and was rewarded with a gush of icy water, which she gratefully allowed to splash across her wrists. In the mirror, her cheeks were flushed, her eyes too bright. Her blonde curls were limp; one had stuck to her forehead and she teased it free, patting her skin with now cool hands. She was in no danger, beyond having slipped into an area of the nightclub she was not meant to explore, and yet her heart was thudding. The frenzied extravagance of the club must be getting to her, she decided. The sooner she found Beth, the better.

In the corridor once more, Harry paused at the bottom of the stairs. Nothing could be heard above the insistent melody from beyond the double doors but that didn't mean anything. She was starting to suspect the club was a labyrinth of hallways and corridors that snaked across more than one building, any one of which might lead her to something she would rather not see. And yet Beth was here somewhere. Could she have gone up these stairs? Gritting her teeth, Harry was about to begin the climb when the double doors opened and someone slipped through.

Harry froze. She wasn't doing anything wrong – she could explain. All she had to do was widen her eyes and confess herself lost.

'My dear Miss White.' Percy's drawl rang with wry surprise. 'Whatever are you doing out here?'

She turned, relieved it was not the gorilla-like doorman they had met on the way in. 'I was looking for the powder room, of course,' she said, hoping she sounded more composed than she felt.

Percy's eyes crinkled in amusement as he came nearer. 'You won't find it up there. Come, I'll show you the way.'

There was nothing for Harry to do but agree, although the realisation rankled. She had no evidence that Beth was in any of the rooms upstairs, but she couldn't eliminate the possibility unless she looked. Unfortunately, there was no way to do that without arousing Percy's suspicions. Stepping back down, she dredged up a smile. 'Would you? That would be awfully kind.'

'Not at all. I wouldn't expect someone as refined as you to understand, but not everyone in a place like this has your best interests at heart.' He paused to glance down at her. 'I'd hate for you to run into anyone... unsavoury.'

Louisa's warning floated into Harry's mind. 'Goodness,' she exclaimed, fluttering her hands in what she prayed was a convincing display of alarm. 'Are the newspapers to be believed? Are there really dangerous criminals here?'

Percy's expression was unreadable and she thought for a heart-stopping moment she had overdone the panic in her voice. But a moment later, he smiled. 'There's danger everywhere, especially after dark.' He slid a chivalrous hand beneath the crook of her elbow, steering her gently back towards the doors. 'Best not to seek it out alone.'

Something in his voice sent a shiver of unease racing along her spine. Both Oliver and Seb had been insistent the Hot Spot was no place for a woman on her own. Had she sent Beth into harm's way? 'Would I truly be in peril if I went up those stairs?'

'Not physically, perhaps,' he said, shrugging. 'But morally? Who knows?'

The anxious clench of her stomach lessened a little. 'I see.'

'Then again, you've always struck me as the kind of woman who isn't afraid to take a calculated risk when the opportunity presents itself.' The smile he flashed her way managed to be flirtatious and unsettling at the same time. 'It's part of what makes you so fascinating.'

Harry thought he must be able to hear the sudden hammering of her heart. 'What have I ever done to make you think that?'

'Nothing at all,' he said. 'But I can't shake the feeling all the same. The trouble is, Oliver Fortescue is determined to prevent me from confirming my theory.'

'That's not true,' she protested, although it sounded unconvincing even to her own ears. Oliver had made it clear he did not trust Percy and he would be glowering like a demon if he could see her now.

They reached the double doors. Percy's black hair was tinged with gold beneath the glow of the light bulb as he turned Harry to face him. 'The last time I stayed at Abinger Hall, I made the egregious error of not kissing you when I had the chance. Do you remember?'

Her mouth suddenly dry, Harry nodded. He was close enough for the scent of cigar smoke and cologne to fill her nostrils. 'Yes.'

A soft smile curved his lips. 'I never make the same mistake twice.'

She should pull away, a distant voice was urging, or tell him she did not want to be kissed. But another, more treacherous part of her was observing that would be a lie. Because his assessment of her was not wrong – she was not afraid to take risks. She revelled in making her own choices, enjoyed the freedom that came from weighing up the odds and deciding for herself whether the risk was worth the reward. And kissing Percy Finchem felt very risky indeed.

There was a loud crash as the door at the top of the stairs banged against the wall. Two women came into view, causing Harry to take a hurried step away from Percy. One was tall and slender, dressed in the style of a dance hostess, beads shimmering dully as she descended. Her blonde hair was plastered to her head in the style of an American gangster's moll. She was, Harry thought, very pretty. The other woman was also tall, but she wore a long satin gown in peacock blue and her dark hair was sleekly styled into a bun. Neither did more than glance incuriously at Harry and Percy as they swept by, their gaze passing over them as though they were pieces of furniture. Seconds later, they had disappeared through the doors.

Harry let out a shaky breath. 'I think I'd like to go back to my brother now.'

Percy's smile was indecipherable as he dipped his head. 'Of course.'

Harry knew two things as she settled once again on the velvet seat next to Seb and watched Percy walk away. One, that she'd come very close to igniting a fire she was not at all sure she could control. And two, the spark was far from extinguished.

7

When Harry awoke the next morning, it was to the ringing of the telephone. At first, she thought it was her alarm clock, but that sat silently on her bedside table, the hands informing her it was seven thirty-seven. By the time it had dawned on her befuddled brain that the shrill bell was coming from the living room, the sound had stopped. She slumped back against the pillow, closing her eyes against the dull ache she knew had been brought on by an excess of champagne and it was little consolation that she had no one to blame but herself. Had she not swallowed a full glass of the stuff in an effort to settle her nerves after her encounter with Percy Finchem, and had she not fallen into bed well after one o'clock the night before, she might feel less dreadful. She had not been drunk but damage had been done all the same. If she hadn't already known that champagne on an empty stomach was a painful mistake, she did now.

A polite tapping on her bedroom door caused her eyes to fly open, before she remembered suggesting Beth spend the night on the settee rather than make the journey back to Camden in the early hours of the morning. 'Hello?' she called.

'It's the telephone.' Beth sounded hesitant, as though she wasn't sure whether she should wake Harry, or even whether she ought to have answered. 'Mr Fortescue is asking to talk to you. He says it's urgent.'

Harry groaned. She hadn't thought to tell Oliver that she had taken the day off work – he probably imagined she was already up and getting ready to set off to Baker Street. 'Could you ask him to wait?' she said. 'I'll just be a minute.'

Yawning, she pulled on her dressing gown and padded through to the living room. Beth was waiting, fully dressed in the clothes she had worn to arrive the day before and holding the receiver in one hand, an apprehensive look on her face. A fire was burning in the hearth and the kettle sat gently steaming on the cooker. The small table had been laid for tea. Harry gaped at her. 'You – I...' Gathering her thoughts together, she tried again. 'You didn't have to light the fire, or make tea.'

Beth bobbed her head. 'It was cold when I woke up and I'm parched.' She held out the receiver. 'Mr Fortescue is waiting.'

Stifling another yawn, Harry took the telephone. 'Hello, Oliver.'

'Who was that I spoke to just now?' he asked, without preamble. 'Have you taken on a maid?'

Harry rubbed a tired hand over her eyes. 'No, that was Beth. It's a long story. What can I help you with?'

'You went to the Hot Spot last night,' Oliver guessed. 'That's why you sound as though you've just been dug up.'

'Yes, Seb arranged it,' Harry said. 'I should have told you, but it all happened fairly suddenly.' She glanced across at Beth. 'We haven't even had time to discuss what we discovered yet.'

'Which means you did uncover something,' he said, sounding intrigued. 'I look forward to hearing all about it.'

Harry felt her cheeks flush as she recalled how close she had come to kissing Percy Finchem. Perhaps there were one or two details Oliver didn't need to know. 'As I said, we haven't compared notes yet.'

'Of course. And I hope you're not too exhausted because I've managed to secure entry to Berkeley Square. My contact suggested this morning, but I thought perhaps after work.'

Instantly, Harry's weariness fell away. 'I can do this morning if you can. I took the day off from the bank.'

'I do have some free time around eleven o'clock,' Oliver said. 'Let me see what I can arrange. Obviously, we'll need to wear our disguises.'

The thought of sticking glue to her overheated skin almost made Harry want to cry, but she had no intention of admitting such a thing. 'Obviously.'

'My outfit is in the carpet bag with yours,' he went on. 'Shall I aim to get to you for ten-thirty? We can get dressed up and make our way to Berkeley Square after that.'

'That sounds like a good plan,' she said. 'Thank you. I'll see you then.'

Hanging up the phone, she fixed Beth with a speculative look. 'I can see you know how to lay a fire and fill a kettle. How are you at sticking on false beards?'

The other woman grinned, not in the least discomfited by the question. 'I expect we're about to find out.'

'But before that, we both deserve tea,' Harry said, touching her head and trying not to wince. 'And perhaps a slice of toast.'

Over breakfast, they shared their experiences from the night before. Harry was able to offer relatively little, although

Beth raised a questioning eyebrow when she heard about Louisa's warning. 'How well do you know this Percy?'

'Not that well,' Harry admitted. 'The Finchem family is very well regarded, and extremely wealthy – his father sits in the House of Lords and his mother—'

'Finchem,' Beth interrupted, frowning thoughtfully. 'Where have I heard that name before?'

'That was the household where my friend Mildred worked as a maid, before she went to Lord Robertson's.' Harry paused. 'It was also the last place Polly Spender was employed, that we know of. But I don't see what any of that has to do with Percy.'

Beth pursed her lips. 'Nothing, I shouldn't think. It's more likely he and Louisa had a fling, and she thought there was more to it. Happens all the time.'

'He's never been anything other than a perfect gentleman to me,' Harry observed, feeling she should defend Percy.

'Because you are a prize,' Beth replied, as though it was the most obvious thing in the world. 'And to men like that, the Louisas of this world are two a penny.'

Harry opened her mouth to object, and closed it again because Beth was quite right. Percy himself might be innocent of the behaviour she had levelled at him, but many more of his status and sex were not.

'Don't lose any sleep over it,' Beth said kindly. 'I expect Louisa was trying to stir up trouble. A woman scorned, and all that.'

'Perhaps,' Harry conceded, because that was a familiar story too. 'Now, tell me more about your adventures. Did you learn anything more about Serafina?'

The other woman looked extremely pleased with herself. 'I done more than that. I met her. And so did you, in a manner of speaking.'

Harry stared at her. 'I beg your pardon?'

Beth grinned, evidently enjoying her moment of triumph. 'When I passed you and Percy canoodling in the corridor, or whatever you was doing. The girl next to me was Serafina.'

She should have known, Harry thought – Beth's companion had clearly been a hostess and she was uncommonly pretty. 'How did you find her? More importantly, how did you get her to talk to you? Did she say anything about Rufus?'

'Slow down,' Beth said, holding up her hands. 'Finding her was a doddle – it helped that I knew her real name. I got chatting to one of the bartenders, told him I was looking for work as a hostess and had been told Ida was moving on. He said she might be willing to vouch for me, for the right price, so I asked where to find her and he pointed me towards the dressing rooms.'

'Which were at the top of that little staircase,' Harry said, putting the pieces together.

Beth nodded. 'I knocked on the door, asked for Ida and there she was, bold as brass and twice as glossy. It took a bit of fast talking for her to trust me but she decided to take a chance when she saw the coin I laid down.'

Harry did her best not to wince. Between Beth's new outfit, the champagne and now this unanticipated expense, their visit to the Hot Spot had been a costly evening, although Seb had footed the bill for the drinks, at least. She had earmarked the money left over from Beth's shopping trip as payment for the work she had done but it sounded as though that had been eaten into. 'What did she tell you?' she asked, hoping it was something useful.

'She said I'd heard right, that she was planning on leaving the Hot Spot,' Beth said. 'Her young man had popped the question and, since he was a man of means, she didn't expect to have to work no more.'

It was just as they had suspected, Harry thought, but it didn't mean Serafina didn't care for Rufus. 'How did she seem when she talked about getting married? Happy? Excited?'

Beth cocked her head. 'I'd say satisfied. Like she'd worked hard and been rewarded.' She stopped, as though replaying the conversation. 'But I wouldn't say she was happy. If anything, she came over a bit blue when she mentioned the wedding. I got the idea she'd been let down before.'

It was interesting information, Harry thought, and certainly seemed to suggest Serafina might be swayed by money. 'Did she happen to say when she expected to be married?'

'Next week,' Beth said. 'By Thursday, it seems, since that's when I'm due to take over her job.'

Harry gawped at her. 'What? You can't be serious.'

'Why not?' Beth replied, shrugging. 'It's good money and I ain't been able to find work anywhere else.'

'But—' Harry broke off as the many reasons Beth should not take a job at the Hot Spot crowded into her mind. 'But Oliver says it's no place for a lady.'

The answering smile was thin. 'I daresay it's not. But I'm no lady, and a job is a job.'

'Come and work for me,' Harry blurted out. 'I can't offer accommodation, but I'll pay a decent wage.'

'For what?' Beth asked doubtfully as she glanced around the neat apartment. 'There's not enough here to keep me busy.'

Harry thought fast. 'As a personal assistant,' she suggested. 'A bit of light housekeeping mixed with digging around and investigating. What do you think?'

Beth still seemed unconvinced. 'Forgive my bluntness, but how much investigating do you actually do? I know Mildred

Longstaff was your friend, so you looked into that case, and obviously Rufus is your brother, but what else do you need me for?'

Harry eyed her pensively, wondering how much to reveal. Beth had proved reliable and resourceful so far, and if she was to be working for Harry, she would have to trust her further. But it didn't follow that she had to share all her secrets at once. Getting to her feet, she opened the drawer where she kept the newspaper clippings of Moriarty's messages, and the articles about the stolen diamond. 'It began on New Year's Day,' she said, laying the newsprint in front of Beth. 'And then it got much, much more intriguing.'

* * *

The policeman on the door of number 48 Berkeley Square had clearly been told to expect the arrival of Mr Thompson and Mr Gill, but that did not prevent him from giving them a stern once-over when they presented themselves. Harry did her best to exude an air of unconcern, while secretly worrying that the padding creating her portly stomach had come loose during the short walk from Hamilton Square. Oliver looked every inch the patrician gentleman detective – the cane John Archer had suggested he use to alter his height worked perfectly – but she had less faith in her own ability to fool anyone trained in the art of observation. It was, however, too late for a crisis of confidence. Steeling herself, she let out a huff of impatience and glared at the officer. 'Come, man, do you think we have all day? Inspector Wells is waiting.'

The mention of his superior had the desired effect. The policeman bobbed his head. 'Of course, sir.'

Turning, he rapped on the door. It was opened instantly,

revealing another uniformed officer. 'Messrs Thompson and Gill, to see Inspector Wells.'

Inside the gloomy wood-panelled hallway, the second policeman appeared less suspicious than his colleague. 'If you'd be so kind as to wait here, I'll let the inspector know you've arrived.'

He disappeared through a door to their right. Harry took the opportunity to study their surroundings. The hall led into three rooms, as far as she could tell – a sitting room of some sort on the left, with two closed doors on the right, the nearest of which had been used by the policeman. One might be a dining room, or perhaps a library, and she surmised the other must be the scene of the crime. The layout was in no way unusual; it was likely that every house in the row had been built to a similar specification. An ornate iron staircase climbed upwards at the furthest end, where she imagined there might be at least one more reception room, along with the bedrooms. Leaning a little to the side, Harry could just make out a fourth door tucked into the wall beneath the stairs. She assumed that led to the kitchens.

'Is Lord Delaware at home, do you know?' she murmured.

Oliver shook his head. 'I believe he is out of town, on pressing state business.'

Harry knew enough of politics to understand what that meant; Lord Delaware was deemed responsible for the loss of the diamond, the repercussions of which rippled all the way to the very top of the British establishment. It was very likely he had been sent away in disgrace, to avoid further embarrassment.

The door opened and the policeman reappeared. Behind him stood a tall, angular woman in a neat tweed suit. 'Inspector Wells,' he said, as the woman strode forwards.

'Mr Gill,' she said in a crisp tone, extending a hand towards Oliver. 'Good of you to come.'

She turned to Harry, who was struggling to contain her surprise. Why hadn't Oliver mentioned that his contact at Scotland Yard was a woman? She knew there were female officers among the ranks of the Metropolitan Police, of course, but she hadn't realised any had risen to the level of Inspector. 'Mr Thompson, ma'am,' she managed gruffly. 'Glad to make your acquaintance.'

Was it her imagination or did Inspector Wells' eyes twinkle as she shook Harry's hand. 'Likewise,' she said. 'Although your reputation precedes you. Mr Gill has told me much of your excellent skill in deductive reasoning.'

Harry shot a look at Oliver, who might have raised his eyebrows beneath the tufts of grey protruding beneath his bowler hat, or might not. He said nothing, however, and she returned her attention to Inspector Wells. Given that Oliver and the policewoman were already acquainted, it seemed probable he had advised her beforehand that he would be masquerading as Mr Gill, although Harry doubted he had divulged the whole reason for the subterfuge. But she couldn't help wondering exactly how much he had revealed about her own identity. 'I do my best.'

The other woman nodded. 'Let us hope you are able to deduce how the Sora-Sora diamond came to be stolen. I freely confess I cannot.' She indicated the open door at her back. 'Please, enter.'

Firing another questioning look Oliver's way, Harry did as she requested and found herself in a grand but unremarkable room laid out as a study. She took a few steps and paused, absorbing the scene. A thickly tasselled Persian rug covered the floor, with a splendidly polished desk sitting in front of a large, unlit fireplace. A window facing out onto the street was on her right, and the wall to her left boasted several rows of bookshelves. In the centre of the shelves hung a magnificent portrait of a man in full dress uniform, which she guessed must hide the safe. 'I see the window is barred,' she said. 'Is this where Lord Delaware routinely stored his valuables?'

Inspector Wells came to stand beside her. 'Yes. The safe contained a number of priceless items at the time of the robbery – jewellery belonging to Lady Delaware, some important papers. None were taken.'

The revelation did not surprise Harry; it seemed obvious that the thief had been intent on one thing alone. 'Not even the tiara that had held the diamond,' she observed. 'A peculiar sort of burglary.'

'Indeed,' Inspector Wells replied. 'That is what makes it so hard to fathom. It's an unusual criminal who leaves most of the haul behind.'

'And Lord Delaware is sure no papers are missing?' Casting her mind back, Harry recalled a number of Holmes stories where vital government plans had been stolen. 'Nothing of political or strategic value?'

'Nothing whatsoever,' the inspector said. 'Just the diamond itself, which is far too recognisable to be sold.'

'Unless broken up into several smaller stones,' Oliver interjected. 'Which would be a crime in itself, given its rarity.'

Frowning, Harry turned in a slow circle, her gaze sweeping the room. 'I understand the door was locked, and guarded all night before the theft.'

'Yes. The guard insists he did not leave his post.'

The painting swung silently back when Harry touched it, revealing a safe that looked both formidable and costly, with a large dial in the centre and a heavy handle to the left. Both were intact and undamaged; no force had been brought to bear to remove the diamond from within. Either the thief had known the combination or they had been an accomplished safe-cracker. Deciding it had told her all it could for now, she crossed to the window and examined the bars, which were likewise sturdy and unbroken. 'No one came through here,' she murmured. 'So how did they get in?'

Inspector Wells smiled thinly. 'If I knew that, Mr Thompson, we wouldn't be having this conversation.'

The ceiling plaster was smooth, Harry noted, with no evidence that the small chandelier had been disturbed. Her gaze came to rest on the Persian rug. 'I assume you have lifted the carpet.'

'Of course.' The inspector inclined her head. 'They did not come up through the floorboards.'

'Then the guard at the door is lying,' Oliver declared. 'It must have been an inside job.'

Wells pursed her lips. 'He is Crown Prince Rupert's own man. The family will not hear a word against him. Not one word.'

But Harry was only half listening. She cast around the room again, her senses primed for the data she knew she was missing. The room was cold, the air tinged with the kind of mustiness that quickly developed in an unheated room in winter. Her eyes settled on the unlit hearth, which she supposed had not been used since the theft had been discovered. But that had been several days ago. Was it strange that the room had not been warmed since then? The desk gleamed, not a speck of dust in sight, and the rug bore no sign of the many pairs of booted feet that must have trampled it over the past few days. Someone had taken care to dust, and sweep, and return things to their usual state. 'When did your fingerprint officers finish their examination?' she asked.

'By Tuesday morning,' Inspector Wells said. 'You may be assured they took extra care to do a thorough job. The only prints discovered were those of Lord Delaware and his domestic staff.'

Harry nodded. She had expected as much. 'I don't see the remnants of powder. Has the maid been allowed to clean?'

The other woman frowned. 'At Lady Delaware's request. I saw no need to refuse.'

Once again, Harry gazed at the fireplace. It was deep and wide, generously proportioned to warm the room with maximum efficiency. Circumnavigating the walnut desk, she knelt to examine the hearth. There was nothing remarkable to be seen – an iron grate swept clean of ash and dust. Above the grate, the chimney was equally broad, narrowing upwards into blackness that left a smudge of soot on her fingertips when she reached into its depths. When Beth had awoken that morning, her primary instinct had been to light the fire and she knew it was the first task undertaken each day by the maids at Abinger Hall.

'If you're imagining that someone came down the chimney, I can assure you they did not,' Inspector Wells said, her tone dry. 'It's blocked by a substantial bird's nest, has been for more than a week. A sweep had been engaged to clear it on Monday and he confirmed no one could have got past it to gain entry. Not without making a considerable mess.'

There wasn't a trace of soot on the cream tassels of the rug, no tell-tale footprint that gave the game away. Harry rapped her knuckles against the solid brickwork at the back of the hearth and accumulated another dusting of black. With a sigh, she placed a hand against the grey stone plinth surrounding the hearth, intending to push herself up, and paused. Given the temperature of the room, and the understanding that the fire had not been lit for over a week, she would have expected the stone to be chilly to the touch. It was not, or at least it was not as cold as it should have been.

'What is it?' Oliver said, noticing her puzzled expression.

Harry pressed her palms flat against the plinth, then ran them across its surface. 'This isn't stone,' she said, and looked up at Inspector Wells. 'It's not cold enough. It feels like wood.'

Reaching into the hearth, she tugged the iron grate out of the way. It slid grudgingly towards her and, as it moved, she saw its feet had dimpled the softer surface upon which it sat. Stretching towards the back of the now empty space, Harry dug her nails into the seam between the wall and the floor, and felt the sliver of a gap. 'Give me a hand,' she said to Oliver, and grabbed the poker from the rack that stood to one side. 'I think there's something underneath here.'

It took several minutes of jimmying with the poker, and a number of muffled curses from Oliver, but at last the wooden board split in two and they were able to pull it out of the way. Beneath it was a wide hole that stretched down into darkness. Harry sat back, sweat trickling through her moustache in a way that was extremely unpleasant, trying not to pant. 'I think we may have found how the thief got in.'

Inspector Wells was gaping at the fireplace in grim astonishment. 'A tunnel. But where does it lead?'

Harry's thoughts flashed to her conversation with Welcome Dobbs the day before. She had thought the information he'd given her might be important and she had been right. 'I imagine they used the old coiners' tunnel that runs beneath the house next door.'

Now it was Oliver's turn to stare. 'How could you possibly know that?'

Harry shrugged the question away. She was not about to give him another excuse to tell her off. 'I read about it,' she said, and looked at Inspector Wells. 'I believe number 50 has recently been renovated and a new family have moved in. It seems to me that such works might provide the perfect cover to dig a tunnel.'

The inspector was eyeing the hole thoughtfully. 'We'll find out when we follow it, although I'm not sure I have an officer small enough to fit inside.'

For an instant, Harry was tempted to volunteer herself, but common sense quickly intervened. Apart from anything else, a man like Mr Thompson would never dream of suggesting such a thing. With some reluctance, she got to her feet and tried to brush the grime from her hands. 'I wish you luck on that score.'

Beside her, Oliver had also risen. 'You'll keep me informed of developments?' he said to Inspector Wells, who nodded.

'It seems your reputation is entirely justified,' she said, regarding Harry with fresh respect. 'Scotland Yard thanks you, although you'll understand if I prefer not to shake your hand at present.'

Something flashed in her eyes then, the same twinkle Harry had observed when they had first been introduced, and she once again wondered just how much Inspector Wells knew about who was beneath the dark whiskers and padding. How had Oliver described her? Someone who should appreciate the nuances of the situation. And Harry supposed he had a point. No one could understand how hard it was to be a woman in a man's world better than a female inspector at Scotland Yard. 'Not at all,' she said. 'I'm delighted to have helped.'

It was a blessed relief to be greeted by a brisk January breeze as they left 48 Berkeley Square, and the light drizzle that began to fall was even more welcome. Harry stared up at the house next door, wondering what the police would find when they followed the tunnel to its end, and what the new occupants would make of their unwitting involvement in the crime that had baffled Scotland Yard.

'You're assuming they're not involved,' Oliver pointed out as they strolled away and she voiced her thoughts.

'I suppose it's possible,' Harry conceded. 'But this crime has been weeks, possibly months, in the planning and I can't imagine Moriarty would be careless enough to leave his accomplices right next door.'

Oliver considered this. 'Probably not.' He walked in silence for a moment or two. 'The discovery of the tunnel will be all over the newspapers when the police reveal its existence. Do you think Moriarty will consider the crime solved?'

She shook her head. 'No. Solving the crime means finding the diamond. The tunnel is only the beginning.'

He sighed. 'I thought you'd say that. So, what's next?'

'Next, we take a regrettably long walk through Hyde Park to make sure we aren't being followed,' she said, and fought the urge to scratch beneath the thick hair that was tickling her upper lip. 'And then we get out of these diabolical disguises. How do you men cope with moustaches and beards? I can't wait to be plain old Harry White again.'

Oliver looked as though he wanted to say something but appeared to change his mind. 'And after that?'

Harry narrowed her eyes as she mulled the question over. 'We need to work out where one might go to recruit a skilled safe-cracker, as well as the name of the builder who undertook the renovations on number 48.' An idea formed in her mind, causing her to smile. 'And then we need to pay him a visit. The good news is that we can remove these dreadful whiskers before we go.'

8

'So let me get this straight,' Oliver said later that day, as they made their way towards the offices of Evans and Long on Kingsway. 'You want us to pose as a married couple who want to renovate their house in Mayfair, for the express purpose of questioning them about the work they undertook at 50 Berkeley Square.'

'That's right,' Harry answered, deciding to ignore the peculiar lurch in her stomach at the thought of pretending to be his wife. 'I think it's the best way to find out if they saw anything out of the ordinary, or whether they were aware of the tunnel.'

He reflected upon this. 'And you're sure it's the right firm?'

'Positive.' In truth, she had been a little taken aback at the ease with which she had tracked down the name of the building company in question – a simple call to Directory Enquiries had provided the telephone number for 48 Berkeley Square, and then she had merely pretended to be calling from the Builders' Amicable Association, checking that the work had been completed on time and to the required standard. This had prompted a long litany of complaints from the housekeeper, which Harry had noted down because it was possible the allegations might come in useful for leverage. Eventually, the disgruntled woman had revealed the information Harry wanted to know – the name of Evans and Long, on Kingsway. It had only been the work of a few minutes more for Harry to find the number of their offices and call, explaining her intention to fully renovate a large house – a house she and her husband had recently inherited after the unhappy death of a distant relative. Money was no object, she assured the secretary, and was rewarded with an appointment at 4.15 p.m. The proximity of Kingsway to the Inns of Court made it easier for Oliver to meet her on the corner of Portugal Street and walk the short distance to Critchley House.

'How do you intend to steer the conversation around to Berkeley Square?' he asked. 'I assume you have a plan.'

'Of course I do,' she said, and patted his arm. 'I'm well aware that you're an expert in the cross-examination of witnesses but I think, in this case, you may leave the talking to me.'

A spark of amusement flashed in his eyes. 'Naturally. Who are we to be for this adventure?'

'Mr and Mrs Dimbleby,' she answered. 'Of 12 Primrose Lane. You are a very successful chartered surveyor and I am extremely well-connected in all the best society circles.'

Oliver grinned. 'That's not actually a lie.'

'No,' Harry admitted. 'But it is important if we want to tease out the truth. Ah, here we are.'

The building was grand and newly built, as were so many others along Kingsway. Once home to slums and some decidedly unsavoury criminal enterprises, the area had been cleared of the ramshackle properties that had flourished during the previous century, and was now a busy thoroughfare that even boasted an underground double-decker tram service running between Waterloo Bridge and Islington. Critchley House hosted a number of businesses, if the brass plaques beside the door were anything to go by. The offices of Evans and Long were on the first floor and Harry was pleased to note she and Oliver did not have long to wait before they were ushered in to see Mr Evans himself. Well-rounded and genial, with thinning hair and small, gold-rimmed glasses perched upon his nose, he shook Oliver's hand and nodded gravely to Harry before waving them into a pair of seats facing a broad desk. Once settled opposite them, he smiled in an encouraging manner. 'Now, we're both busy men, Mr Dimbleby, so let's get down to business.' He glanced at Oliver. 'I understand you have a substantial property you wish to be modernised. Is that correct?'

Oliver nodded. 'That's right. But it's my wife you should be addressing. The property is hers.'

Mr Evans glanced at Harry. 'I see.' He paused to clear his throat and recalibrate his approach. 'Might I ask about the condition of the property now?'

'It's structurally sound,' she said, the words deliberately crisp. 'The renovations will be to the interior – there are several inconvenient walls I would like removed and the staircase is most disagreeable.'

The builder's smile grew a little condescending. 'We may not be able to remove all of the walls, madam. They often serve a vital purpose in holding the building up. Staircases are likewise a necessity.' He aimed a conspiratorial look at Oliver, who did not return it. 'Not something I'd expect a lady like you to understand but there may be some room for compromise.'

It was exactly the response Harry had expected. She arched an eyebrow. 'Compromise? Your firm comes highly recommended by a number of wealthy friends and acquaintances, Mr

Evans. Am I to understand that these recommendations were unwarranted? That you cannot undertake the renovations we require?'

He blinked. 'No, not at all. I'm sure we can accommodate your requirements, Mrs Dimbleby. As long as it's safe to do so.'

She sat back, her expression suggesting she was far from convinced. 'Have you much experience of restoring Georgian properties? Perhaps if you can describe a recent renovation in London, we may feel reassured.'

Evans licked his lips. 'But of course. We've not long completed work on a house in Notting Hill that went very well.'

Harry favoured him with a wintry look. 'Notting Hill.'

The builder picked up on her evident disapproval. 'And there was another in Berkeley Square, for a Mr and Mrs Anderson. That required substantial rebuilding but I think I can safely say they were pleased with the results.'

Harry tapped her fingers together. 'Anderson,' she repeated. 'Would that be 50 Berkeley Square?'

'Yes,' Mr Evans said, looking surprised. 'Do you know the family?'

She turned to Oliver. 'Didn't the Andersons invite us for dinner last month?'

'If you say so, my dear,' he replied vaguely.

'They did. And then they were forced to cancel, because the building works had overrun. Mrs Anderson was simply beside herself, do you remember?'

Oliver made a non-committal sound as Mr Evans threw Harry a worried look. 'There were some delays, now you mention it, but I hardly think they can be blamed on my workers. We did an excellent job, under the circumstances.'

Harry's gaze sharpened. She folded her hands in her lap. 'What circumstances?'

The man ran a hand over his chin. 'I'm not sure I should say.'

With a sniff, Harry rose. 'A bad builder blames his clients, Mr Evans. Thank you for your time.'

'Wait,' he exclaimed, a look of panic crossing his face at the thought of losing a potentially lucrative client. 'I suppose it won't hurt to tell you.' His gaze travelled back and forth between them as Harry sank back into the chair, and he sighed. 'It was a straightforward job at first. The house was empty, meaning we didn't have to worry about disturbing the family. There was a manservant of sorts, who oversaw the work, and a maid who stayed in the attic rooms and made tea when we needed it. But they mostly left us to it.'

'How much work was required?' Harry asked, thinking of the rat catcher's assertion that the house had been unoccupied for years.

'Oh, it was a big job,' the builder replied. 'Damp from the roof, plaster falling off the walls, woodworm in the floorboards, particularly on the first floor. Several of the bedrooms were uninhabitable. But we're hard workers at Evans and Long, and we got on with it.' He hesitated, clearly trying to decide how much to reveal. 'After a day or two, some of the men started to complain about the atmosphere in the house. Obviously, it was a bit gloomy – it was winter, after all, but it was more than that. They said it felt as though they were being watched – a couple of them even complained about tools going missing. I told them to pull themselves together.'

'You didn't believe them?' Harry asked, recalling Dobbs' claim that terrible deeds had occurred inside the building. Perhaps there was a sinister air to the place.

'I did not,' Evans said firmly. 'Mr Long and I thought it more likely they were on the take, pawning the tools and claiming they'd simply disappeared, even though they'd always been reliable lads up until then. But it got worse – we went in one morning to find everything gone.'

Oliver leaned forwards. 'All of your equipment had vanished?'

'Not vanished, exactly. Just moved around the house, as though someone was playing tricks on us.' He shook his head. 'The manservant insisted he and the maid had nothing to do with it and I couldn't see why he would lie. The men got right jumpy after that – claiming the floorboards had suddenly started creaking, strange sounds coming from the walls, that kind of thing. One of my best lads lost his head completely and insisted the dining room was three feet smaller than it had been the week before. A few refused to work there at all. We had to recruit replacements, which set us back and delayed completion of the work.' Licking his lips, Mr Evans sent a nervous grin across the desk. 'But we got the job done and I'm sure your house won't present any such peculiar complications.'

'No, indeed not,' Harry said, injecting the words with as much distaste as she could muster. 'Tell me, did your men find any evidence of any tunnels beneath the house?'

The builder's eyebrows shot up. 'Tunnels? Whatever do you mean?'

'Between the adjoining properties,' Harry explained. 'A friend told me she discovered something of that sort when she took on a house in Mayfair and found it to be infested with rats, and it turned out they were coming through the chimney from the house next door.' She paused to offer a delicate shudder. 'I cannot bear rats.'

Understanding dawned on the man's face. 'We checked the chimneys at Berkeley Square as part of the renovation – all were sound. We can do the same for you, Mrs Dimbleby. All part of the service.'

She nodded and aimed a covert glance at Oliver, who rubbed his hands together. 'Most reassuring, Mr Evans, I can see why your services are recommended. I think we've heard enough.'

The other man glanced between them. 'You're leaving? But we haven't discussed the details of your—'

'All in good time,' Oliver said, jovially. 'I'm afraid we have another appointment now, but if we decide to go ahead with the work, we will most certainly be in touch.'

Harry summoned up her most disarming smile. 'Thank you so much for your honesty. Good day, sir.'

Neither she nor Oliver spoke again until they were standing on the pavement outside Critchley House. Oliver eyed her curiously. 'Well, it was a very interesting meeting but I'm not sure we learned anything useful. What was all that nonsense about their tools? Are we meant to believe the place is haunted?'

'I don't know,' Harry admitted. 'But it's not the first time I've heard of strange things happening in that house. I'm afraid it has rather a dark history.'

Crossing the road to Keeley Street, she repeated the gruesome tale Welcome Dobbs had shared with her.

'So that's how you knew about the coiners,' Oliver exclaimed. 'But I still don't see how any of that relates to the theft of the diamond.'

They had reached Wild Street and paused to cross. 'I'm not sure it has anything to do with it,' she conceded. 'But if Mr Evans' men are to be believed then it seems obvious to me that something else was going on during the renovation of 50 Berkeley Square. The tools did not move themselves. Perhaps they were being put to other uses overnight.'

Oliver cocked his head. 'Uses like digging a tunnel between houses?'

'Possibly,' Harry said, and frowned. 'I don't see how that was done without anyone at number 50 noticing, however. I wonder if Inspector Wells has made any progress in finding out where it leads.'

A car chugged past, leaving the road clear. Harry stepped off the pavement and was immediately jostled by someone. She felt a tug at the pocket of her coat and looked down to see a ragged girl at her side. 'Sorry, missus,' she mumbled, head down. 'I slipped.'

She made to skip away but Harry was too quick. 'Not so fast,' she said, shooting out a hand to grip the girl's bony wrist.

The child looked up in alarm and began to wriggle. 'Get off! Get off me!'

Her fearful shriek almost made Harry let go, just as a memory surfaced in her mind. 'Wait a minute, I've seen you before,' she said, tightening her fingers. 'A few nights ago, near the Garston Club. You were trying to work out how to pick my pocket.'

'Wasn't,' the girl said defiantly, but the wriggling lessened and Harry thought her eyes were slightly less wary.

'You were,' she said. 'I left a coin on the bench. Did you find it?'

With obvious reluctance, the girl shrugged. 'Yeah.'

Oliver glowered at her. 'And you decided to repay this generosity by picking her pocket again.'

This elicited another shrug. 'Didn't know it was her.'

Harry studied her thoughtfully. 'I think you did. I think you realised I had money to spare and decided to help yourself to some more.' She paused. 'Unfortunately for you, the pocket you chose is empty.'

'I know that,' the girl snapped sullenly. 'So you can't hand me over to the police. I ain't stole nothing.'

'You tried,' Oliver pointed out. 'That's illegal too.'

The wriggling resumed. 'Let me go! My mum lives just over there – she'll flay you alive if she hears me yelling.'

Harry hesitated. The girl was even thinner than she had suspected from their last encounter, and younger too – perhaps only seven or eight. Her cheeks were gaunt beneath their layer of dirt and there was a sunken look to her eyes. Was she really about to hand such a poor creature over to the police? What good would it do? She gnawed at the inside of her lip, weighing the decision up. Perhaps there was another way. 'I have a shilling for you if you promise not to run.'

Instantly, the girl's wriggling stopped. She eyed Harry with evident distrust; a shilling was a lot of money to a child who had very little and she had done nothing to earn it. 'Why would you do that?'

'I want to ask you a question,' Harry said. 'Don't worry, it's nothing that will get you into trouble.'

The girl scowled. 'That's what they all say.'

It was probably best not to think too much about that, Harry decided. With slow deliberation, she released the girl's wrist. 'I'm sorry if I hurt you,' she said, watching her rub the skin. 'I'm going to reach into my bag now, and get the money. See?'

She held up the silver coin. The girl stared back at it, suddenly mesmerised. 'What's the question?'

Harry held up a hand. 'A few preliminaries first. What's your name?'

This was met with another ferocious scowl but the girl kept her attention on the prize. 'They call me Midge.'

'Midge,' Harry repeated, and thought it suited her somehow. 'How old are you?'

'Eight.' There was a truculent pause. 'Almost nine.'

'Thank you,' Harry said. 'And do you really live around here?'

Midge jerked her head. 'Yeah. That's my school, just over there. Wild Street School.'

Both Harry and Oliver looked up and saw an austere, red-bricked building that looked more like a prison than a place of education. 'I see,' Harry replied. She did not want to consider the kind of education that the pupils of such an establishment might receive.

'That's three questions,' Midge said, and snatched at the coin. 'Can I go now?'

Harry jerked her hand out of reach. 'One last matter. You look like a clever girl who knows all kind of interesting things. The kind of things they don't always teach you in school. Am I right?'

Midge appeared torn between wanting to agree and the instinct to grab the money and run. 'Depends. I ain't much good at sums.'

Harry fought the urge to smile. 'I'm not going to ask you to add anything up,' she said, and lowered her voice. 'But I do want to ask you this. If I wanted to find the best safe-cracker in London, where would I start looking?'

'A peterman? What do you want one of them for?' The girl's expression grew wary again. 'Are you coppers?'

'Not at all,' Harry said, guessing the word peterman was slang for a safe-cracker. 'But if you don't know the answer then that's fine.'

'Of course I know,' Midge scoffed. 'You want Middlesex Street. Solomon Pole, the pawnbroker.'

The name meant nothing to Harry, but the street rang a faint bell. Where had she heard it before? 'Middlesex Street. Where's that?'

'Petticoat Lane,' Midge said. 'Over east. That's where I'd go, anyway.'

Of course, Harry recalled. That was where Beth had gone to procure her outfit for the Hot Spot; presumably the area was home to much more than just good-value seamstresses. She smiled at Midge. 'Thank you, that's very helpful.' She was about to hand over the coin when another thought occurred to her. From time to time, Holmes had made use of street children to convey messages and find out information he couldn't. Perhaps this was another opportunity for life to imitate art. 'Is this your patch, Midge?' she asked. 'Where you... work, I mean?'

The girl did not reply, and Harry supposed she could hardly blame her. 'What I'm getting at is, can I find you here if there's ever anything else I want to ask you?' She flashed the coin. 'There could be more of this on offer, if you're able to help.'

Midge stared at her for a long time, as though taking her measure, then nodded. 'Yeah. Around here or in Covent Garden.'

Harry held out the shilling. 'In that case, you may well see me again. As long as you promise not to pick my pocket next time.'

Grabbing the coin, Midge bit the edge to check it was real. 'I'll try not to.' The shilling vanished into the grubby recesses of her clothing as she squinted up at Harry. 'One other thing. Solomon Pole is bad news. Don't mess with him, or them that works for him. It won't go well if you do.'

With that, she whirled around and tore off along the street, disappearing around a corner before either Harry or Oliver could say another word. 'Why do I have the feeling you're already planning a trip to Petticoat Lane, in spite of our new friend's warning?' Oliver rumbled as they began to walk again.

'Of course I am,' Harry said, tutting. 'But if it makes you feel any better, I won't go alone. Beth is familiar with the neighbourhood, she'll make sure I don't stumble into anywhere I shouldn't.'

Turning the corner into Long Acre, Oliver looked very much as though he were about to argue, but the words appeared to die in his throat as they were confronted by a newspaper stand. 'Read all about it – murder in Mayfair! Body found in Berkeley Square. Read all about it!'

Harry stopped dead, her hands flying to her mouth in dismay. Oliver strode forward, thrusting some money at the seller and snatching the evening edition from the stand. He brought it back to Harry and they both stared at the headline.

THEFT TAKES A DEADLY TURN
BODY FOUND IN MAYFAIR MANSION

'It's number 50,' Harry said numbly, scanning the tiny newsprint beneath the awful heading and absorbing what little detail there was. 'My God, Oliver, what does it mean?'

'I don't know,' he replied, his tone grim. 'It could just be a terrible coincidence.'

Harry searched his face, her stomach swooping with anxiety. 'You don't believe that.'

'I don't know what to believe,' Oliver said, and folded the newspaper under his arm. 'Come on. I need to talk to Inspector Wells.'

9

It was almost eight o'clock in the evening when Harry's telephone finally rang. She had been trying to finish the Dorothy L. Sayers novel she was reading but the words would not stay still on the page and she found it impossible to keep track of the plot. In the silence, the phone was shrill enough to make her jump. She scrambled to answer it. 'Hello?' she said breathlessly into the receiver. 'Oliver, is that you?'

'Yes, it's me.' His voice thrummed with tension. 'Are you alone?'

It was not a question she'd been expecting. 'Um – yes. Beth and I have agreed that she'll start her official duties on Monday, although we've arranged to meet near Middlesex Street tomorrow morning. Why?'

'I've spoken to Inspector Wells,' he said, the words flat. 'I – well, it's not good, Harry. Not good at all. There's no doubt that the death is linked to the diamond.'

She let out a gasp. 'But how?'

'I don't have all the details yet but it appears Inspector Wells found a chimney sweep's boy willing to follow the tunnel beneath the fireplace,' Oliver said. 'It led under the foundations of the house and into a small sealed chamber with no other way in or out.'

Harry blinked. She had expected the tunnel to link up with that of the coiners, perhaps leading out into a neighbouring street. 'But that makes no sense. How did the thief escape?'

'First impressions suggested they did not,' Oliver replied. 'The room contained the body of a young woman. It appears she has been there for several days.'

The revelation caused Harry's stomach to swoop in horror. Various terrible scenarios played out in her mind and all were the stuff of nightmares. 'The poor sweep's boy.'

'I gather he was quite fascinated,' Oliver said, his tone droll. 'He claimed it was the most exciting thing that had ever happened to him.'

Having grown up with three brothers, Harry could easily believe that but it did nothing to lessen the awfulness of the discovery. 'Have they been able to identify the body?'

'Not yet. There are a number of other troubling aspects,' he went on. 'As I mentioned, the room was sealed when the body was discovered and it is not clear how the young woman came to be there.'

Harry frowned. 'Obviously, she hid there to steal the diamond and then for some reason was unable to make her escape.'

'There are two problems with that,' Oliver said. 'Firstly, the diamond was not in the room with her and there is some doubt she could have navigated the tunnel in order to steal it. And secondly—' He broke off, giving Harry the distinct impression he was gathering himself to say something he feared would upset her. 'Preliminary examinations indicate she did not die there.'

Harry felt a shudder run through her as she forced herself to consider the possibilities. 'Whatever do you mean? Surely the poor girl suffocated? Or – or starved to death.'

'Her neck was broken,' he said, with flat practicality.

'Then she must have fallen,' Harry reasoned, her imagination flooded with yet another unbearable scenario. 'Probably in an effort to get out. Was there anything in the room she might have climbed upon?'

'Yes, there was a chair,' Oliver said, and sighed. 'She was tied to it.'

Harry closed her eyes. She had very little experience of corpses but she suspected few tied themselves up to await discovery.

'There's something else,' Oliver said, and he sounded even more troubled. 'She didn't have the diamond but there was something in her hands. A letter addressed to Sherlock Holmes.'

It felt to Harry as though the floor fell away then. She clutched at the telephone table for support. 'To Holmes?' she repeated, as the implications came thick and fast. 'But that means – it suggests...'

Abruptly, she stopped speaking but the name Moriarty tightened around her like the coils of a serpent. 'There are a lot of unanswered questions,' Oliver said gently. 'I don't think we should rush to any conclusions without a better understanding of the letter's contents. Inspector Wells has agreed to show it to us, in exchange for any insight we – that is to say, you – are able to offer into these new developments.'

A dull roar began to build in Harry's ears. The letters she read and replied to in the course of her work at the bank had often involved accusations of murder, but they had always seemed remote and fantastical, and she had not judged any of them as likely to be true. This letter could not be so easily dismissed. Someone had gone to terrible lengths to get Holmes' attention and she could not shake the horrifying suspicion that the death of this unfortunate girl was somehow her fault. Perhaps, had she acted on her instincts sooner, the girl might still be alive. 'When?' she asked, as guilt threatened to overwhelm her. 'When can I read it?'

'The inspector wants us at the house as soon as possible,' he said. 'Within the next hour, if we can manage it.'

'It will take us that long to get dressed,' Harry observed, running a shaky hand across her forehead. 'And we don't have Beth to help with our whiskers.'

'I daresay no one will notice if they are not quite symmetrical,' Oliver reassured her. 'Will you be all right until I get there? I should be with you in about quarter of an hour.'

She didn't answer right away; her head spun with the shock of the revelations. Murder – for it seemed that could be the only explanation – changed everything. 'Of course,' she managed at length, in a voice that did not sound like her own. 'I'll see you soon.'

She sat without moving for several minutes. Slipping into the role of Sherlock's secretary had never felt like a game to her – she had always been too aware of the real-life consequences that hung on her actions, for both those who sought help and for Harry in supplying it – but the knowledge that murder had finally made a chilling appearance made her blood run cold. Yet even as she replayed the shocking conversation with Oliver in her mind, common sense reasserted itself. She had not dealt the blow that killed the girl, nor had she done anything to trigger it. The terrible impulses that drove some to kill was as old as time, as was the determination of others to bring their victims justice. Whoever the dead girl turned out to be, and whatever the reason for her demise, the best Harry could do for her now would be to help find those responsible for her death.

Giving herself a brisk shake, she went into her bedroom and pulled the carpet bag from under the bed. By the time Oliver arrived, she had laid their disguises out and set the kettle on the stove. A cup of Earl Grey could not wash away the distress she still felt, but perhaps it might ease things a little.

The look Oliver gave her when she opened the door was penetrating. 'How are you feeling? Bearing up?'

She managed a nod. 'Yes, I think so.'

Oliver did not look convinced. 'Because you don't have to do this if you don't want to. I know you're strong, Harry, but murder is a grim business. I wouldn't blame you in the slightest if you decided to leave matters to the police.'

Grim was exactly the right word, Harry thought, even as she shook her head. 'If it wasn't for the letter then I might be tempted to do just that.'

'We don't know for sure that it's from Moriarty,' he countered.

She did not grace that with an answer. 'Have we got time for tea, do you think?'

He eyed her for a long moment, then gave up. 'I think so, yes. It's probably going to be a long evening.'

* * *

The pair of stern-faced uniformed officers at the door of 50 Berkeley Square did not surprise Harry in the least, nor did the two burly figures that loomed outside number 48. This time, she and Oliver were not kept waiting on the doorstep; the door was open before they could even give their names and they were waved inside without ceremony. Inspector Wells met them in the hall, her expression sombre as she shook their hands. 'We'll start in here,' she said, indicating the door to the study. 'I have a few questions before we address the worst of this business.'

The room had been significantly reordered since Harry and Oliver had last visited. The curtains were now drawn, blocking the view to and from the street, which she assumed was to prevent ghoulish onlookers and members of the press from gawking at the scene. The desk had been moved to one side and the tasselled rug was rolled up, revealing dark wooden floorboards beneath, some of which had been lifted here and there in an effort to ensure there were no further tunnels. A large white sheet covered the area in front of the fireplace, criss-crossed with muddy bootprints. The hole in the hearth was guarded by a uniformed officer, who saluted as Inspector Wells approached. 'Would you mind giving us a moment, PC Vincent? Close the door on your way out.'

When they were alone, she turned her brisk gaze upon Harry. 'Has Mr Gill explained the situation to you?'

'I believe he has covered the essentials,' she replied cautiously. 'A secret chamber was found at the end of the tunnel, and this chamber contained the body of a young woman.'

'Exactly so,' Inspector Wells said. 'I'm sure he has also informed you of the letter we found, somewhat bafflingly addressed to someone who does not exist.'

'Yes,' Harry said, resisting the temptation to fire a covert glance at Oliver. How much did Inspector Wells know?

'Needless to say, we have not released that particular detail to the public.' Her eyes sharpened. 'Sherlock Holmes. If I didn't know better, I'd suggest it was an extremely tasteless joke.'

Ah, Harry thought, with a sinking heart. She knew. 'I wish it was.'

The other woman sighed. 'I'm sure you do. But the time has come to lay our cards on the table, Mr Thompson. When I was first approached by our mutual friend, Mr Fortescue, he explained your position to me.'

Harry did not dare look at Oliver. 'Oh? What position is that?'

'He advised me that, for the purest of reasons, you had investigated several crimes under the guise of an assistant to Sherlock Holmes,' Inspector Wells said. 'In the course of these investigations, it would appear that you have made a powerful enemy. Someone who has attempted to draw you out, but who also enjoys toying with their prey before they pounce. Someone who calls themselves Moriarty.'

There seemed little point in denying it. 'Yes,' Harry said simply.

'Very well,' the inspector replied. Crossing to the desk, she picked up an envelope and thrust it towards Harry. 'Then this is yours. I hope it means more to you than it does to me.'

They had opened it, of course, and Harry had no doubt it had been subjected to a number of forensic tests; a shimmer of silvery powder still adhered to the envelope. With some trepidation, she withdrew the letter and began to read.

My dear Holmes,

RxP+

Yours in expectation,

Professor James Moriarty

Harry had to hand it to the author; once again, it was a perfect encapsulation of the dynamic between Moriarty and

Holmes, a carefully considered game of intellect and skill. It did not matter that the stories of Arthur Conan Doyle had never featured such a contest – the message was clear. When she looked up, she found both the inspector and Oliver watching her closely. 'It's a chess move,' she said. 'Rook takes Pawn – check. He's telling me that the game is almost over. If I don't neutralise the threat, my King will fall.'

Oliver's expression darkened. 'By Pawn, I assume he means the dead girl.'

Folding the letter up, Harry returned it to the envelope. The casual cruelty of the reference had not been lost on her and it took some effort to extinguish the flare of anger it caused. 'Yes.'

'Despicable,' he muttered.

Inspector Wells cleared her throat. 'The reason I asked you to come here with such urgency is that we have not yet removed the body. I wonder if you might be willing to look at her, in situ, as it were. There may be something you see that we do not.'

'I'm not sure Mr Thompson needs to do that,' Oliver said, stepping forward. His eyes met Harry's, and she saw they were dark pools of concern. 'I cannot imagine the victim was known to you.'

As ever, he meant to protect her and, for once, Harry almost wanted to let him. She had no desire to be confronted by a dead body, and certainly not one that had been waiting at least five days to be found. But it would not do to turn away now, not when it seemed obvious that the young woman's death was being used as a ghastly taunt. Without knowing her identity, it was impossible to determine whether the victim had been a confirmed criminal or an innocent caught up in Moriarty's web, but the fact remained that she had lost her life, while those responsible were still at large. Could Harry continue to look at herself in the mirror each day if she turned away without doing her utmost to help catch them? 'Do you need me to go through the tunnel?'

Inspector Wells widened her eyes. 'Oh, no. Didn't I tell you? The room isn't underground. We discovered there was a false wall in the house next door. Two of my officers broke it down as soon as the body was found.'

Harry exchanged an astonished look with Oliver. 'The renovation work,' she exclaimed. 'Didn't Evans say his men heard strange noises in the walls?'

'Yes. And one of them claimed the dining room had shrunk.'

'The dining room?' Inspector Wells repeated sharply. 'That's where the false wall is.'

Harry took a deep breath. 'I think perhaps you'd better show us, Inspector.'

'Follow me,' she said. 'Understandably, the Anderson family is not there at present. They've gone to stay with friends.'

As Harry had anticipated, the layout of 50 Berkeley Square mirrored its neighbour. The hallway was less gloomy, the paintwork fresher, but the configuration of rooms was exactly reversed. On the left of the front door was the room the Andersons had been using to dine in. A splendid mahogany table had been pushed aside, the chairs piled untidily on top. But it was the wall furthest from the door that immediately drew Harry's gaze: a large ragged gash had been opened up in its centre, the intricately patterned gold and green wallpaper dangling in fronds around the edges. Like its counterpart next door, it was guarded by an impassive policeman. Inspector Wells nodded to him as he handed her a torch, then stepped back to give them room. 'You'll need this,' she said, turning to Harry and Oliver. 'Which of you wants to go first?'

Before Harry could speak, Oliver took the torch. 'I will.'

With grim determination, he switched on the beam and disappeared through the hole. 'There's no smell,' Harry observed, wrinkling her nose at the absence. 'If she's been here since the diamond went missing, shouldn't we be able to smell something?'

'Ordinarily, yes,' Inspector Wells said. 'But that's the other thing that led us to understand she didn't die here. The body has been embalmed.'

'Embalmed?' Harry echoed, feeling her forehead crease in bewilderment. Embalming was a skilled undertaking, performed only by those in the business of handling the dead. 'What – how—?'

The inspector shrugged. 'I can only assume it was to ensure the body wasn't discovered before the thieves could escape the country with the diamond. As for the how – our medical staff tell me it's quite common for funeral directors to visit private homes for the purposes of embalming a corpse before burial.'

Harry raised her eyebrows. 'Even when the body has a broken neck?'

'I imagine a lot of money was paid for the embalmer to ignore that inconvenient fact,' Inspector Wells said, her expression darkening. 'Or perhaps they were coerced into helping. Either way, they are unlikely to come forward if we put out an appeal.'

Harry could not fault her logic. 'Finding out who the victim is might help,' she said, as the torchlight flashed beyond the hole in the wall.

'It would certainly be a start,' the other woman allowed. 'But I don't expect they gave the embalmer her real name, or any other identifying details. They're too clever for that.'

A few minutes later, Oliver reappeared in the gap, his face ashen. 'She's not much more than a child.'

His obvious distress caused Harry to swallow. But she had come too far to back out now. Waiting until he was clear of the hole, she held out her hand for the torch. In silence, she pressed the switch and stepped through the jagged opening.

She deliberately did not look at the body in the chair, knowing it would snatch the breath from her lungs. It made more sense to assess the scene first, take in the details she might miss once her thoughts were clouded by emotion. Moving the torch beam across the floor, she observed the sawed-through floorboards in one corner and the yawning black depths of the tunnel beneath. The space was narrow, less than three feet across, and stretching the length of the original dining-room wall. Far above, the ceiling was smooth and white, but it didn't appear to bear a coat of plaster like its neighbour, which suggested the hidden room had been constructed before the plasterer had completed his work. Other than the tunnel, and the rough hole that had been hacked into the false wall, there was no way in or out. Involuntarily, she glanced at the girl's feet, which were neatly encased in black Mary-Janes. How had she come to be here? Harry wondered. If it was not for the rope that bound her to the chair, she had the appearance of someone waiting patiently to see the dentist. With a sigh that caught in the back of her throat and threatened to become a croak, Harry raised the beam of light to play over the dead girl's face. Immediately, the torch tumbled from her hand.

She didn't realise she had screamed until Oliver barged into the space to grip her hand. 'What is it? What's wrong?'

Wide-eyed and gasping, Harry could barely manage to breathe. Oliver stooped to collect the torch, turning its light onto the body once more. With an immense effort of will, Harry wrestled her thundering heart under control and heaved in an enormous, shuddering breath. 'It looks like... I think it's

Polly Spender,' she said, through lips that were clumsy and thick. 'The missing girl from Southwark.'

Oliver swore. Inspector Wells appeared in the gap, her expression solemn. 'Are you sure?'

Steeling herself, Harry gazed at the still, lolling head and summoned up a memory from Lady Finchem's sitting room months earlier, when the maid had served them tea. She'd been nervous, her eyes darting from side to side and her hands shaking as though terrified of doing the wrong thing, but Harry was certain the horribly lifeless features and mouse-brown hair she saw now belonged to the same girl. 'Yes. I only met her once, but I'm sure it's her.' She looked away as another cruel thought occurred to her. 'P for Polly.'

Inspector Wells stared at her. 'I beg your pardon?'

'I assumed it meant Rook takes Pawn, but it could also have meant Rook takes Polly.'

Oliver nodded in bleak understanding. 'You always suspected she was involved in the robbery at the Finchem house. It seems entirely possible she's here because she got dragged further into that criminal underworld.'

Harry averted her gaze from the sad shape in the chair. 'I... Do you mind if we go back into the dining room?' she said, swallowing to dislodge the hard lump that was forming in her throat. 'I'd like some air.'

Oliver offered his arm and she took it gratefully as she picked her way through the gap.

'The first step will be to confirm the girl's identity,' Inspector Wells said, once the three of them stood in the dining room once more. 'I'll have someone interview the Spender family and take matters from there. Did you notice anything else that stood out? A clue that tells us how she came to be here?'

'Not immediately,' Harry said, as her pounding heart began settle. 'Perhaps the other thieves sealed this wall after placing her here.'

The inspector considered this. 'The Andersons held a dinner party the night the theft occurred. They say this room was in use until almost midnight, a claim that has been corroborated by the household staff. The family took breakfast here the following morning and did not notice anything amiss, nor did they observe any disturbances during the night.'

Harry found she did not care to look at the gash in the wall and fixed her gaze upon the floor. The theft of the diamond had been an intricate crime, months in the making; how many had played a part in it? There was the thief who had taken the stone – someone small enough to squeeze through the tunnel yet skilled in the art of safe-cracking and nimble-fingered enough to remove the diamond from the tiara. There was Polly herself, although it was not clear what her role had been. Harry narrowed her eyes. There must have been at least one other, perhaps two, because Polly had not walked into the secret room – she had been carried there once dead and tied to the chair. The envelope had been tucked into her hands, to await discovery. And the entire endeavour had been undertaken with the utmost quiet. It seemed unlikely in the extreme that the perpetrators had also managed to seal the wall and restore the fussy wallpaper immediately after the theft, least of all with such skill that it was undetectable to those who lived in the house.

'Then the wall is not the answer,' she conceded, and recalled the lifted floorboards in the study of number 48. 'I assume you've checked for other tunnels.'

'That was my first thought too,' Inspector Wells said. 'Your talk of old coiners aroused my suspicions and my men were able to locate the tunnel you mentioned. It was thoroughly blocked and we found no evidence of any others.'

Harry turned to Oliver, who met her gaze steadily but offered no solution. 'I confess I'm at a loss,' she said at last. 'For the moment, I can't see how it was done.'

Inspector Wells sighed. 'Nor can I. There is also the mystery of how the false wall came to be constructed in the first place. We'll need to question the builder who oversaw the renovation.'

At that, Harry felt her stomach tighten. Mr Evans would undoubtedly recall the couple who had been so interested in the work at 50 Berkeley Square and perhaps might mention it to the police. The watchful expression on Oliver's face suggested he had arrived at the same realisation. 'We are a little ahead of you there,' she said. 'Some associates of ours had occasion to visit the building firm in question – Evans and Long – yesterday afternoon, and took the opportunity to ask about the renovation. It seems there were some unusual aspects to the job.'

Briefly, she outlined everything they had learned from Mr Evans. If Inspector Wells understood who exactly had visited the builder, or found it strange that they had anticipated the need to question him, she did not say so. She merely absorbed the new information. 'He may remember more when interviewed by Scotland Yard,' she said, and smiled in a manner that made Harry glad they were on the same side. 'People often do.'

'I'm curious about the caretaker and the maid Mr Evans described,' Oliver put in. 'Are they still part of the household staff?'

'We asked Mrs Anderson about any changes in her domestic arrangements,' Inspector Wells said. 'The caretaker was called Noah Cooke. He applied for the job in answer to a newspaper advert placed by the family and came highly recommended, with impeccable references. When the work was completed, he left the Andersons' employ. I've sent an officer to his last known address to see if he has returned there.'

Whoever Noah Cooke was, his presence throughout the duration of the renovations, along with his prompt departure the moment they were complete, suggested he might well be complicit in the construction of the tunnel that led to number 48, as well as the secret room, Harry thought. It was hard to imagine how either could have been achieved without him noticing. 'And the maid?' she asked.

Inspector Wells frowned. 'Mrs Anderson didn't mention a maid. She said the caretaker occupied the house alone.'

Oliver eyed her soberly. 'You may want to ask Mr Evans about that. I imagine his workers will be able to give you a description of the girl they claim to have seen.'

The inspector's eyes flicked to the hidden room. 'You think it was Polly Spender.'

'I wouldn't dream of speculating without evidence,' Oliver replied. 'But it's possible, wouldn't you say?'

Once again, Harry felt a flutter of sadness at a life cut short. From the little Beth had shared, it seemed Polly Spender hadn't had much of a start in life. 'Poor girl.'

There was little more to be said after that. Harry and Oliver took their leave, promising to inform Inspector Wells of any further communications from Moriarty. Once again, they took a circuitous route back to Hamilton Square, the suspicion that they must be observed and perhaps followed preying on Harry's mind. Connections were materialising with alarming speed: between the theft of the Sora-Sora diamond and the robbery for which Mildred Longstaff had been framed, between the investigation Harry had undertaken and Holmes, and Mr Longstaff's encounter with the man claiming to be Mr Spender, and between the shadowy criminal organisation Harry had been warned had people everywhere and the man calling himself Professor James Moriarty. It seemed impossible that they had not been observed entering and leaving the houses on Berkeley Square, but if they were being followed, their pursuer was very good. Once or twice, she thought she caught sight of someone in the shadows, but she couldn't be sure it was not the product of her overheated imagination. Even so, an excess of caution would do no harm.

As they passed along Bury Street, a small queue clustered beneath the glow of Quaglino's caught her eye. She tugged on Oliver's sleeve. 'I don't know about you, but I could use a drink.'

His gaze followed hers and came to rest on the queue. 'In there?' he said doubtfully. 'We don't have a reservation.'

Harry checked the time – almost eleven o'clock. Was it too much to hope that Seb was inside? 'I think we might be able to bluff our way in,' she replied in a low voice, resisting the urge to glance over her shoulder. 'When we reach the front, follow my lead.'

Thankfully, the queue moved fast. As before, John Quaglino himself was at the door, greeting his customers with enthusiastic cheer. His eyes narrowed slightly when they fell upon Harry and Oliver, and she supposed they did not present themselves as typical guests of the establishment. Plastering on a wide smile, she thrust out a hand. 'Quaglino, my good man, how the devil are you? Capital to see you again.'

John Quaglino's gaze flickered over the guest list and back to Harry, clearly trying to place her. 'All the better for seeing you, my friend,' he said, warily shaking her hand. 'But I was not expecting you this evening. Remind me, under whose name is your reservation?'

'Sebastian White, of course,' Harry said, crossing her fingers that the gamble would pay off. Surely her brother would not be sitting at home on a Friday evening. It was a reasonable bet that he was here. Quite what he would make of her clothing was another matter entirely but that would only become a problem if he was as predictable as she hoped.

Once again, the man consulted his list. Harry held her breath and sensed Oliver's raised eyebrows, although he had followed her instructions not to say a word. It would not be the end of the world if they were turned away, but it would be mildly embarrassing and likely to excite a comment or two from at least some of those behind them. 'Ah, yes,' Quaglino said, and cocked his head. 'Is he expecting you to join his party?'

Harry hesitated. The difficulty was that Seb hadn't the faintest idea she and Oliver planned to join him, and he most certainly was not expecting two heavily bearded gentlemen in distinctly drab suits. She suspected John Quaglino was far too wise to allow them inside without verifying with Seb first, and he would not recognise the names of Mr Thompson and Mr Gill. It was time to shed those identities, if not their camouflage. 'It's a spur-of-the-moment visit,' she confessed. 'But if you advise him that Harry White and friend have arrived, then I'm sure he'll be overjoyed to see us.'

The man surveyed them both again, and Harry tried not to squirm as his attention rested on the awful wig sprouting out from beneath her hat. 'One moment, please,' he said, and murmured to one of the burly men stood discreetly at his shoulder. The man disappeared inside and Mr Quaglino turned back to fire a charming smile at Harry and Oliver. 'If you wouldn't mind stepping aside.'

'Are you sure this is a good idea?' Oliver whispered as they waited. 'I'm not sure what will happen if I try to remove this hat.'

'We'll keep them on,' she replied. 'People will stare but we'll look so out of place that they're going to do that anyway.'

He regarded her levelly. 'Then why are we doing this?'

She sighed. 'Because I think someone might be following us. No, don't look.'

Oliver had the grace to look sheepish. 'Sorry. But won't they just hang around until we come out?'

'I had a thought about that,' she replied. 'But let's see if we get in first.'

A few minutes later, the doorman returned and spoke to John Quaglino. He turned to Harry and Oliver, beaming widely. 'Mr White is delighted you're here. Please, come in.'

The cloakroom attendant could not hide her consternation when both guests declined to remove their hat and coat. 'But you'll be dreadfully warm,' she said, her expression suggesting they had taken full leave of their senses.

'Don't trouble yourself, my dear,' Harry rumbled, sliding a shilling towards her. 'We're not staying long.'

The bar was busier and the band much louder than on Harry's previous visit. She wished she had a camera to capture her brother's expression when she and Oliver were escorted to his table by a blank-faced waiter. Seb rose, gaping in bewilderment as he stared from one unknown face to the other. 'Good to see you again, White,' Harry boomed, clapping him on one shoulder. Leaning closer, she reverted to her natural voice. 'Sit down, you fool. It's me.'

His eyes widened in almost comical astonishment, but to his credit, he recovered fast. 'Wonderful of you to join me,' he managed, and sank into his chair. He waved at two of the empty seats clustered around the table. 'Won't you sit? What will you have to drink?'

'A Manhattan,' Harry said firmly. 'Make it a strong one.'

'Whisky,' Oliver said, and puffed out his cheeks. 'Make it quick.'

Seb peered at him, his incredulity growing. 'Fortescue? Is that you?'

With obvious reluctance, Oliver nodded. 'Hello, Seb.'

Laughter exploded across the table, causing several heads to turn in their direction. 'Good lord. For once, I think I might be lost for words.'

Harry leaned back in her chair, wishing she had followed the suggestion of the cloakroom attendant and left her coat upstairs, if not her hat. She was far too hot and those around them were making no attempt to hide their curiosity. She fanned herself with the cocktail menu. 'It's a long and complicated story but don't worry, we can't stay long.'

Her brother nodded. 'I'm very glad to hear it. Lord and Lady Pritchard are joining me soon and I cannot begin to fathom how I would explain the two of you.' He studied Harry with interest. 'Is that a dead ferret on your face?'

'Behave yourself,' she hissed. 'I borrowed it from Drury Lane, if you must know.'

Seb's expression lifted. 'You're involved in a drama? That makes sense, although I can't imagine how you've managed to persuade Fortescue to get involved.' He turned an amused look towards Oliver. 'Who are you meant to be? Old Father Time?'

'Mr Gill, actually,' Oliver said, a little stiffly. 'Sidekick of the great detective, Mr Emmanuel Thompson.'

'Excellent,' Seb said, and raised his glass of champagne. 'I never had you down as the dramatic type, but you must let me know when your opening night is coming up. I'd be delighted to come and support you.'

'I will,' Harry said, battling to keep her own expression neutral. 'But for now, I need your support with something else. Tell me, is there a back door here?'

'But of course,' Seb replied. 'How else would they remove those guests who have partaken in too much merriment at the end of the night? It's through the cellars.'

Harry nodded. 'Do you think we might use it to leave?' Her brother's eyebrows rose. 'It's for the play. Method acting – the art of experiencing, as the eminent Mr Stanislavski calls it.'

She had read about Konstantin Stanislavski and his school of acting in one of her mother's magazines and she hoped it would lend some much-needed credibility to her story now.

'Who am I to argue with such dedication?' Seb said, with airy respect. 'Although I think you should know I don't believe a word of it. What are you really up to, Harry?'

She was saved from having to answer by the arrival of the waiter with their drinks. Once he'd gone, she took a fortifying gulp of her cocktail and opened her mouth to reply, but Oliver beat her to it. 'It's my fault,' he said, shooting Seb an apologetic look. 'One of my contacts at Scotland Yard gave me a lead on Serafina Eccleston and I persuaded Harry here to go undercover to follow it up.'

It was all Harry could do not to drop her drink and Seb appeared similarly astonished. 'Undercover? I must admit, I didn't think you had it in you, Oliver. But I appreciate the lengths you're going to on our behalf. That wig is a crime all on its own.'

'So now you see why we need to use the back door,' Harry said, flashing Oliver a grateful look before turning an entreating gaze upon her brother.

'Not really,' he said. 'But discretion is all part of the service here.' Raising a hand, he summoned a waiter and murmured something into his ear. The man nodded and straightened, turning an expectant look towards Harry and Oliver. 'Drink up,' Seb went on encouragingly. 'Lord Pritchard is coming down the stairs and I really don't care to introduce you.'

Obediently, Harry swigged the rest of her cocktail, wincing as the alcohol seared its way to her stomach. 'Thanks, Seb,' she said, rising to follow the waiter. 'I owe you.'

He waved her away. 'Don't mention it,' he said, his expression somewhat pained. 'Really, don't mention it. I dread to think what Mama would say. Let's just pretend this never happened.'

The waiter maintained a dignified silence as he led them through the sea of whispering diners, towards a discreet burgundy velvet curtain and a set of stone steps beyond it. The air grew noticeably cooler as they travelled further underground, for which Harry was profoundly grateful. They passed a number of alcoves, each piled high with pyramids of wine bottles that looked dustily expensive. At last they came to another staircase, leading steeply upwards to a door. Without a word, the waiter drew back a number of bolts and pulled the door open, fixing his gaze somewhere above the lintel. Offering a nod of thanks that she knew would go unacknowledged, Harry stepped past the man and onto one of the narrow alleyways that ran between some of Mayfair's streets. Rectangles of light shone at each end but the alley itself was black with shadows.

A resolute thud indicated the door had been closed behind Oliver. 'Now what?' he said.

Harry stood still for an instant, savouring the bite of frosty air and the welcome anonymity of the night. She had been all too conscious of the attention they had garnered as they had made their way between the tables in Quaglino's. It had been a relief to be able to pass beyond the velvet curtain and an even greater respite to escape the mute disapproval of the waiter escorting them. But they could not linger in the passageway forever. 'Now we go home. Separately.'

Oliver shook his head, as she knew he would. 'Absolutely not.'

'It makes sense,' she argued. 'If whoever was following us is still in the area, they'll be looking for two men, not one.'

He folded his arms. 'If you think I am letting you walk home alone at almost midnight, then you don't know me very well at all.'

His glower almost matched hers in ferocity. Harry raised her chin. 'I appreciate that you mean well, Oliver, but you have to stop treating me like a child. You only see me as your best friend's little sister but I'm a fully grown woman. Haven't I proved I can look after myself?'

Oliver's jaw tightened. 'Believe me, I'm well aware of everything you are, Harry. And I don't think of you as Lawrence's little sister.' He stopped and looked away. 'Perhaps it would be easier if I did.'

'What does that mean?' she cried. 'Easier to do what?'

He took a deep breath. Harry waited, fists clenched in frustration. She was tired of having to bend to society's expectations, tired of being told what she could and could not do. And right at that moment, she was tired of Oliver's overcautious attitude. She was wearing a false beard and a suit, for goodness' sake, she looked every inch a man, especially under cover of darkness. What could possibly happen to her in the ten minutes it would take to walk to Hamilton Square?

'Easier not to care,' he said.

He meant for her reputation, Harry supposed, and huffed with irritation. 'No one is going to recognise me dressed like this.'

'I don't imagine so,' he replied. 'But that isn't what I meant. Everything would be easier if I didn't care for you.'

Abruptly, the wind was plucked from Harry's sails. 'You... care for me?'

The look he gave her was level. 'You must know I do. Would I be dressed like this if I didn't?'

'But—' she paused to gather her scattered thoughts '—you're dressed like that to solve a crime – to make sure justice is done.'

Oliver shook his head impatiently. 'I'm dressed like this because you asked me to. The same way I pretended to be a workman and was almost killed by an angry mob in south London, and waded through freezing fenland to follow a boat in Cambridgeshire. I wouldn't do all of that for just anyone, Harry.'

It was true – she had demanded he do both of those things and much more besides, and the realisation made her queasy with guilt. She had asked too much of him, put him in danger, both physically and professionally, and used his friendship with Lawrence to persuade him to risk everything. Her head drooped as she stared at the floor. 'I'm sorry.'

'Why should you be sorry?' he said, his impatience subsiding into bafflement as he sighed. 'I can see I'm going to have to speak plainly and it would really help if you could look at me while I do.'

Reluctantly, she raised her head, bracing herself for the painful truth. His face was half hidden by the shadows, but she saw the glitter of his eyes as he observed her.

'Thank you,' he said, and cleared his throat. 'I can't claim this is exactly how I imagined saying this but, for the avoidance of doubt, I am not here out of a sense of duty to the law, or your family, or anything else. I am here because of you. Because I can't get enough of the way you light up when you piece together a puzzle, or make a connection no one else has noticed. Because I see how much helping people matters to you, especially when the law fails to do so. Because you are kind and resourceful and determined and brilliant, and every time I think you can't surprise me more, you do.' He took a breath. 'Because whether I'm crouching in a cockroach-ridden hovel, or up to my neck in icy water, or bundling into a dingy alley behind a nightclub wearing a beard that itches like sin, there's no place I'd rather be, as long as I'm next to you.'

It was the longest speech she'd ever heard him make, and for a brief moment, she contemplated how impressive he must be in court. But the undisguised admiration in his voice made her blush, and she was very glad for the darkness that meant he could not see it. She managed a guarded nod. 'As my lawyer and my friend.'

'Well, yes, of course. But I actually meant as more than that,' he said. 'If... if that's what you want.'

The uncertainty that laced his last sentence made her breath catch. This was Oliver – cool, logical, lawyerly Oliver, who she had never known to be unsure about anything until now. She'd always believed he had been oblivious to her teenage adoration and, until she had approached him for help last year, had shown only polite interest towards her when they had encountered one another. Which made this sudden declaration all the more disconcerting.

'I...' she said, and trailed off because the way he was looking at her made it hard to think.

Stepping nearer, Oliver gently tilted her chin upwards and searched her face. 'Is that what you want, Harry?'

His eyes glistened blacker than midnight as they fixed on hers. He was going to kiss her, she thought, and the realisation caused her doubts to scatter, replaced by a thrill of anticipation that threatened to collapse her knees. After all this time, Oliver Fortescue was going to kiss her and, once he did, nothing would ever be the same again. All she had to do was say yes.

'Here! What's going on down there?' A brusque voice caused Harry and Oliver to spring apart in alarm, their faces whipping towards the end of the alley where the shadow of a man loomed. 'Don't you know there's laws against that? Disgusting, unnatural behaviour!'

The accusation made no sense until, with a jolt, Harry recalled how they were dressed. A surge of indignation rose inside her. Love was love, no matter who it touched. 'Then the law is an ass!' she called back defiantly.

'Is it now?' the man roared, and she saw two more bodies appear to block out the rest of the light. 'We'll just see about that.'

Oliver gripped her arm. 'Time to go,' he urged, drawing her towards the other end of the alley. 'Now, Harry!'

He was right, of course, but that didn't mean Harry enjoyed conceding the battle. Reluctantly, she turned on her heel and ran, her booted footsteps echoing like machine-gun fire on the stone slab pavement. Behind her, she heard Oliver breathing hard, and heavier footsteps thundering behind him. She flew out of the alley, spun to her left and raced across the road to Cork Street, ignoring the frantic beep of a horn and the gasps of those hardy revellers who were still out and about. Drawing in a frantic breath, she took a right, then a left along Old Burlington Street. Another right took her onto Boyle Street; she could sense Oliver at her shoulder but the thud of their pursuers seemed to have faded. With a burst of speed, she dashed across Savile Row and up towards Mill Street.

'Harry!' Oliver puffed at last. 'Harry, it's okay. They've given up. We're safe.'

She slowed, glancing over her shoulder and beyond him to the empty pavement behind. 'Are you sure?'

'I don't think they made it past Boyle Street.'

Panting, she straightened her hat and dabbed at the sweat beading on her upper lip, willing the burn in her lungs to dissipate. 'Fine. But we shouldn't stay here. They might turn up at any moment.'

Oliver studied her for a moment, then nodded. 'Agreed.'

She found she couldn't quite meet his gaze, all too aware of what had almost happened in the alley, before the men had seen them and the need to escape had eclipsed everything. 'Oliver, I—'

He held up a hand. 'Don't say anything. I know how much you value your independence and I'd never ask you to give that up. But I take nothing back. I do care for you, Harry. If you decide that can only be as your friend and your lawyer, then that will have to be enough.'

She closed her eyes. How many times had she wished he would say such things to her? Yet now that he had, it was all too much. Perhaps it was simply the timing; the day had been overwhelming, with the discovery of Polly's body, the realisation that the two investigations she had been pursuing were bound by a deadly silken thread, and unexpectedly culminating in a panicked chase through the streets. Or perhaps it was simply that everything was different now. She was different now, and romance – any romance – came with a price, one that would inevitably clip her wings. There would be positives, of course;

at some point she might grow tired of life on her own, especially if she loved and was loved in return. But there was no denying that, for a woman, love and all that followed was a gilded cage. And Harry did not want to be caged. Not even by Oliver.

A sudden wave of exhaustion hit her with the strength of a storm surge, and she found she didn't have the fortitude to examine her own heart. All she wanted was to fall into the soft oblivion of her bed. 'I'm going to go home. Please don't argue, it's only a few streets away.'

To his credit, he did not insist on accompanying her. 'Will you call me once you're there?'

In spite of her weariness, Harry smiled. He really couldn't help himself. Never mind that she would be home long before he was and that it would mean delaying her own rest to reassure him. But she supposed she still had to remove her disguise, and the whiskers would take time. 'Of course.'

He smiled back. 'Speak soon, then.'

She dipped her head, and wished for one contrary moment that he would walk her home. 'Speak soon.'

10

If Harry had been able to get a message to Beth in time, she might have postponed the visit to Petticoat Lane on Saturday morning. Despite the exhaustion she felt when she had finally reached her bed at almost one o'clock, she hadn't slept well. Remorse over Polly Spender's untimely death, combined with the irrational guilt that she had somehow contributed to it, had kept her restless and staring at the ceiling. When she had slept, her dreams were plagued by a shadowy figure chasing her along endless streets, with Oliver and Beth begging her to run faster, and it did not take the brilliance of Sigmund Freud to determine that her nightmares were born of the very real fear that Moriarty was on her tail, and might target one of her associates if he caught wind of who they were. Oliver was already in danger, having publicly represented Mildred Longstaff, and Beth's visits to the Spender family might mean she was at risk too. It meant Harry had eventually risen with a dry mouth and a dull ache in her temples that aspirin did nothing to alleviate. Her fingers were clumsy and slow as she dressed herself as Sarah Smith, dulling her blonde curls with boot polish and adopting some of John Archer's stage make-up techniques to give herself subtly sunken cheeks and a wan complexion. The drabness of her appearance matched her spirits as she took the Underground to Liverpool Street station.

Beth was waiting for her on the corner of Frying Pan Alley. The other woman surveyed Harry with a narrowed gaze as she approached. 'You look how I feel,' she said with a sniff of disapproval. 'Don't tell me you've been burning the midnight oil again.'

Harry hesitated. She had spent most of the journey from Bond Street wondering how to tell her about Polly. 'In a manner of speaking.'

Beth studied her shrewdly. 'I take it that means yes. Still, at least them bags under your eyes help you look the part. Did you bring something to show?'

Nodding, Harry reached into her pocket and pulled out a silver charm bracelet laden with intricate charms. 'Very nice,' Beth said, brushing a tiny carriage with the tip of a gloved finger. 'Not too flashy but worth a fair bit. It should keep them busy at the counter while you get a feel for the place.'

This was the plan they had hatched together – Beth would present the bracelet to the pawnbroker and haggle over the price, while Harry gave the shop a discreet once-over. She wasn't sure what she expected to find – if the thieves were connected to Solomon Pole in some way then the Sora-Sora diamond would hardly be in plain view. But it was a place to start, if nothing else, and she might discover something she could report to Inspector Wells. 'Just to be clear, this bracelet belonged to my grandmother as a child. I don't actually want to pawn it.'

Beth grinned. 'Don't worry. They'll offer a low price, I'll pretend to be offended, maybe try and get them to offer a bit more. Then we can sweep out in high dudgeon and nip away sharpish before they twig we were wasting their time and send the heavies after us.'

'The heavies?' Harry repeated, fragments of her unsettling dreams flashing across her thoughts. The pounding of monstrous feet upon the pavement had felt all too real.

'I expect there'll be at least one,' Beth said, her tone matter-of-fact. 'To make sure no one gets any ideas about taking the law into their own hands. Pawnbrokers come in handy if you're short of ready cash, but I can't say anyone likes them much.'

That was understandable, Harry supposed. She had no experience of such things but she was well aware that some people were only too happy to exploit those with little money. Knowing they had their customers over a barrel meant a pawnbroker could offer less than an item might be worth and demand much more to repay a loan settled on it, meaning it could take a long time for a much-loved treasure to be reclaimed. And if the pledge was not repaid within the time agreed, the item became the property of the pawnbroker, to display and sell in the shop. It seemed only natural to Harry that such custodians of hope and heartbreak were not especially popular, just as it was perfectly reasonable that they might feel the need for security, but Beth's words still caused her stomach to churn. They needed to handle this reconnaissance mission with caution. 'Let's get on with it.'

Petticoat Lane market did not operate on Saturday, so Middlesex Street was not thronged with stalls and traders the way it would be the following day. The shops that lined the road were still doing a brisk trade, although Harry saw several that were boarded up, clearly out of business. The windows of one had been plastered with posters, many of which were promoting unemployment protests and hunger marches.

Others advertised must-have products or outlandish entertainments. Harry's gaze lingered on a garish, eye-catching jumble of images proclaiming the marvels of Cuthbert's Travelling Circus, which appeared to have set up at London Fields and boasted 'mighty elephants, ferocious lions and a most rare and elegant unicorn'. It certainly sounded marvellous, she thought. Hadn't Patrick the doorman mentioned visiting one in East London with his family? 'I see the circus is in town,' she observed, pointing the poster out to Beth. 'Have you ever been?'

'I went last year,' she said, with a dismissive glance at the red-cheeked ringmaster exhorting them to roll up. 'The unicorn's horn fell off right away, but the acrobats were good. It made me want to learn the trapeze, until I realised there's no safety net. You'd have to be mad.'

Harry eyed the poster more closely and spotted a small drawing of a young woman in a plumed yellow costume, seemingly flying through the air unaided. A sad, white-faced clown peered mournfully from one corner, while a strongman lifted a colossal barbell, grinning as though it was nothing. It appeared that Mr Cuthbert had plenty of attractions to boast about. 'Oh,' she said, when she noticed the dates emblazoned along the bottom. 'There are two shows today, but it closes tomorrow.'

'They never stay in one place for long,' Beth replied. 'A week, perhaps – ten days at most – and then *poof*. They're off to the next field or park, up and down the country.'

She wiggled fingers to suggest a magical disappearance but something was nagging at Harry, an elusive thought that danced in and out of her mind, tickling at the edges of her consciousness. After spending a moment or two trying to catch it, she gave up. 'Oh, that is a shame,' she said, sighing. 'I think I might have enjoyed the trapeze artist too.'

Beth shook her head. 'Oh, it ain't for the likes of you. The seats are cheap to attract them as won't think too hard about what's in front of them. You'd see through the illusion in a heartbeat, and it's all tatty and clapped out underneath.'

It was the closest Beth had ever come to giving her a compliment, but it made Harry feel a little mean-spirited, as though she lacked the imagination to embrace the magic. She certainly did not feel particularly sharp at that moment. Moriarty was running rings around her, Rufus still planned to elope with a woman they knew next to nothing about, and she had no idea how she was going to respond to the near miss – the near kiss – with Oliver the night before either. In the cold light of day, she wondered whether she might have dreamt his heartfelt declaration. It had been so very out of character. Could he really have meant the things he said? It seemed impossible and yet he had taken extraordinary risks to help her. Would he do such things if he didn't care for her?

'There it is,' Beth cut into her thoughts, nodding across the street to a black-fronted shop that had seen better days. A bar supporting three brass balls hung over the door, the traditional symbol for a service that catered mostly to the desperate and destitute, and the windows were filled with a forlorn array of mismatched items that made Harry's spirits droop. A prettily dressed china doll leaned against a chamber pot, a leather-bound bible sat next to a violin, and a silver-tipped walking cane lay in front of them. There were multiple pairs of children's boots in different sizes, and a well-made greatcoat pinned to a mannequin. As Harry crossed the road and drew nearer, she saw several dusty racks of jewellery.

'I should have brought something more eye-catching,' she fretted, noticing there were numerous bracelets adorning the faded velvet cushions, amid clusters of watches and gold rings.

'And I'm glad you didn't,' Beth replied with her customary

bluntness. 'We'd have been robbed blind before we got halfway back to the station. Now, when we get inside, keep your mouth shut. I'll do the talking.'

Harry did not argue. Sarah Smith's accent was passable enough in some parts of the city, but she doubted anyone from the East End would be fooled for long and she didn't want to give the game away before they had even begun to play. She reached for the door handle. 'Ready?'

'As I'll ever be,' Beth replied, and winked. 'In we go.'

The tinkle of a bell over the door announced their arrival and it took a moment for Harry to adjust to the gloom inside. The shop was smaller than she'd expected, and decidedly Victorian in style. The floorboards might once have been polished but were now dusty and scuffed with the passage of many boots. Dark, wood-panelled walls held shelf after shelf of clutter, everyday items that had once been treasured, reluctantly given up and lost. A glass-topped counter took up almost the entire length of the far wall, with additional goods on display in its depths – the more valuable stock, Harry assumed, spying jewellery, silver candlesticks and a canteen of cutlery. A large ledger rested in the centre of the glass top, open to a page that was filled with line after line of handwritten scrawl; the record of debtors, she guessed. It was presided over by a tall, thin man with deep-set eyes that roamed across the two of them with the kind of naked calculation that made Harry's skin crawl. She could not escape the feeling that they had stepped straight into the den of a Dickensian arch-villain. 'Ladies,' he said, smiling in a manner that held more than a hint of a crocodile assessing its prey. 'What can I do for you today?'

Glancing at Beth, Harry saw that a curious change had come over her since they had entered the shop. Gone was her cheerful confidence, replaced by a timid look of shame that almost caused Harry to blink in surprise. 'Are... are you Solomon Pole?' she asked, her voice wavering and subdued.

'At your service,' the man said, and Harry saw his gaze narrow in greedy anticipation even as his smile widened. 'How may I help?'

Thrusting her hand into her pocket, Beth withdrew the silver bracelet. 'What'll you give me for this?'

Solomon Pole's gaze fixed upon the glittering chain dangling from her tightly clenched fingers. 'Come closer, my dear. No need to be scared, I'm here to help.'

Beth did as he commanded, but not before she cast a swift look at Harry. That was her cue, she realised, and she turned away as though uninterested in the tawdry financial transaction that was about to occur. She allowed her eyes to roam the shelves, not focusing on their contents but taking in the strategically angled mirrors fixed to the walls that allowed whoever was standing behind the counter to watch out for light-fingered visitors. There was no sign of the brutes Beth had predicted but a beaded curtain covered a doorway in the wall to the rear of the counter. Perhaps they were lurking in there.

From the corner of her eye, she saw Beth had relinquished the bracelet. Solomon Pole was bent over it, an eyeglass held between long spindly fingers as he studied the delicate charms attached to the links. Harry had no idea of its value in monetary terms; each charm had been hand crafted from the finest silver, soldered into place with seamless skill, a new one added for birthdays and anniversaries and other celebrations over many decades. Its sentimental worth was beyond price, but it seemed it was also a prize worth having, if the expression on Solomon Pole's face was anything to go by. Harry did not intervene, however. Beth knew her task well enough. She resumed her study of the shop. Now that she was closer, she saw that the trays of jewellery beneath the counter contained pieces that were clearly of higher quality than their neighbours. A gold signet ring embossed with the kind of seal she associated with the nobility, although no one sealed their letters with wax any more. An emerald pendant set on a fine gold chain that glimmered even in the dimness. A jewel-handled knife that was far too beautiful to be of any practical use. Harry frowned. These were not the possessions of the working class, hastily exchanged for too little money and never reclaimed. These were something else.

'I see you have an eye for the finer things,' Pole said, and Harry looked up to see him watching her.

'I like stuff what shines,' she said, and decided to take a risk. 'I suppose you might say I collect it.'

'We have that in common,' he said. His tone was bland but she thought he took her meaning. 'Is that how you came by this particularly fine piece?'

Harry shook her head. 'Nah. That's hers, handed down through her family.' She paused. 'But I reckon I might come across one or two shiny bits and bobs to add to your collection, from time to time. Stuff what don't match my own interests, if you catch my drift.'

From the warning look Beth flashed her way, Harry suspected she was talking too much but if her accent was imperfect, Pole did not seem to notice. He resumed his inspection of the charm bracelet. 'I run a respectable business here – all above board.'

'I can tell,' Harry said, and cursed the error in judgement. 'I didn't mean to suggest otherwise.'

'And yet I have a weakness for the finer things myself,' Pole went on. 'Perhaps we may be of use to one another after all, Miss—'

Her heart thudded. 'Peterman,' she said, as coolly as she could manage. 'Hilda Peterman.'

He lowered the eyeglass to observe her then. 'Peterman,' he repeated, as Beth also glanced at her sharply. 'An interesting surname. Tell me, is it the family occupation?'

Harry tried a carefree shrug. 'No. But I'm always on the look-out for long-lost family members. Maybe you know one or two.'

He regarded her for several seconds. He was no longer a predator surveying its prey – now his manner was that of a scientist contemplating an interesting specimen. 'It's possible a Peterman might be found in my ledger,' he said. 'But there are so many names.' His attention switched suddenly to Beth, who had been following the exchange with narrowed eyes. 'I'll give you half a crown for this.'

Her mouth fell open in what Harry thought was genuine outrage. 'What? It's worth ten times that.'

He shrugged. 'You say it's a treasured family heirloom but how am I to know whether that's true? Half a crown is a fair price for something that might bring the police to my door, wouldn't you say?'

Beth scowled. 'It ain't stolen.'

Pole inclined his head. 'Perhaps not, but the risk is mine nonetheless. My commission on the loan will be a further half-crown, bringing the total pledged to a full crown. You have one year and a day to repay the pledge, starting from today's date.' His hand closed around the bracelet. 'Do we have an accord?'

'That's robbery!' Beth said, and her voice rose several notes. 'No, we do not have an accord. I'll go and see Mrs Hackett, she'll give me a better price.'

A distant scraping sound broke the silence that followed her words. Harry heard the ponderous tread of heavy feet. The beaded curtain swayed and rattled as a meaty fist appeared and forced the strands apart. 'They giving you trouble, Mr Pole?'

The man was a giant, Harry thought as he ducked through the doorway to glare at them. His shirt strained over enormous biceps as he folded his arms, and she saw his forearms were covered in tattoos. The face was florid and wide, its size only exaggerated by his bald head. His eyes were piggy, dwarfed by a large hooked nose that looked as though it had come off worse in a number of fights. The overall impression was of a mountain that had pulled loose from the earth, but there was intelligence in his porcine gaze and Harry was struck by a fleeting observation that he was somehow familiar to her, although she was certain they had never met. He was, however, exactly the kind of complication she had feared. She exchanged a look with Beth and something passed between them. There was no help for it, Harry realised as she smothered a wave of dismay. They would have to agree. 'All right, you've got a deal,' Beth said. 'Mind you don't sell it. I'll be back for it as soon as I get myself straight.'

Solomon Pole reached for the ledger. 'A wise decision. I'm going to need your name and address for my records.'

Harry tensed. They hadn't discussed providing a false address, not having planned to get as far as pawning the bracelet. But Beth showed not a flicker of concern as she reeled off the name Lizzie Devine, and an address in Bethnal Green that might be real or as fake as her name. If Pole was suspicious, he didn't show it. His bruiser radiated menace as Pole handed Beth a numbered ticket. 'You need this when you come to pay. I won't release the item without it, no matter how much you beg.'

Beth studied the ticket, then squinted at the ledger. 'Does it match what you wrote down there?'

Pole turned the book to show her. 'As I said, Miss Devine, I run a respectable business.' His gaze flickered to Harry. 'And perhaps if you both return, I may have had time to consult the ledger for that long-lost family member you mentioned.'

Harry said nothing as he slid a coin across the glass towards Beth. 'I hope that helps to alleviate your financial difficulties,' he said smoothly. 'Good day to you both.'

The giant took a step forward, making it clear the transaction was at an end. Glowering at both men, Beth snatched up the money and flounced to the door. Harry followed, resisting the temptation to cast a longing glance at the bracelet. They would retrieve it, she told herself as an ache welled up in her chest. It was not lost. Overhead, the bell tinkled and was abruptly cut off by the closing door. Neither of them spoke. Instead, they set off along Middlesex Street, listening for the thud of heavy feet that suggested trouble was brewing.

When they reached the derelict shop adorned with posters, Harry placed a hand on Beth's arm. 'I think we're safe.'

'I'm not sure we are,' Beth grumbled, but she stopped walking all the same. She held out the ticket and the half-crown to Harry and sighed. 'I suppose these are yours.'

'Keep the money,' Harry said, taking the ticket. 'As payment for today.'

Beth looked as though she might refuse, then tucked the money away in a pocket. 'So now what? I'm sorry about the bracelet. I know it's important to you.'

Another stab of dismay pierced Harry's stomach, but she forced herself to ignore it. 'That's not important for now. What matters is that we've established Pole isn't against handling stolen goods.'

The other woman sniffed. 'Hardly the discovery of the century.'

'No, but there's also the suggestion that he knows a safe-cracker or two,' Harry countered.

'I did wonder where you were going with all that long-lost family malarkey,' Beth said. 'But then I remembered that Peterman is another name for a safe-cracker. That was quite clever, even if it did bring the plan tumbling down around our ears.'

'Yes,' Harry admitted. 'Sorry about that.'

It had been a risk, but one that had been worthwhile, she decided. And perhaps the odds had always been against getting out of the door with the bracelet still in their possession. It certainly seemed that Solomon Pole had meant to have it. Her gaze came to rest once more on the poster for Cuthbert's circus and she stared without really seeing it, her mind circling around everything the pawnbroker had said.

'At least we didn't get beaten black and blue,' Beth cut in, sounding a little more positive. 'Did you see the size of that devil he had working for him?'

'Hmmm,' Harry said absently, as something tugged at her memory. Her gaze slid across the poster, taking in the grinning strongman with his bulging forearms, and something fell into place. 'Beth, look at this. Do you think that's him?'

'What, the bruiser? It can't be.' Squinting, she followed Harry's pointing finger. 'I bet they all look the same – big, ugly and stupid.'

Harry leaned closer. 'But look at those tattoos. There's one of a mermaid on his left forearm – I saw that back in the shop. And the anchor on his right arm. Pole's bruiser had one of those too.'

'Could be coincidence,' Beth said, but she sounded uncertain. 'Maybe he's an artist's muse.'

Harry's mind was whirring. Her eyes slid to the picture of

the acrobats, small and lithe. 'What if there's a connection between Pole and the circus?' she said slowly. 'The job at Berkeley Square needed an expert safe-cracker, but it also needed someone small enough to navigate the tunnel.'

Beth's gaze settled on the acrobats. 'There was a little one,' she said, as though recalling a distant memory. 'No more than a kid. You think the circus is involved with the theft of the diamond?'

'Perhaps,' Harry said, although the idea sounded ridiculous even to her ears.

'I suppose it's possible,' Beth allowed, then frowned. 'Hang on, didn't I see in the papers that they found a body in that house?'

Harry felt all the adrenaline from the morning's adventures drain away like water from a sink, leaving her empty and heart-sore. She looked around for a bench where they might sit or, better yet, a public garden that might take the sting out of what she had to say, but she saw neither. In the distance, she spotted what appeared to be a pub, and checked her watch. It was almost opening time; with a bit of luck, they might even get a table and a modicum of privacy. At the very least she could take some gin to fortify herself.

'Where are we heading now?' Beth asked, falling into step with her. 'Ain't you going to answer my question?'

'Yes,' Harry said, and wished all over again that she didn't have to reveal such awful news. 'But I think we're both going to need a drink before I do.'

11

Beth took the news of Polly Spender's unhappy end in silence, her lips pressed tight as though she did not trust herself to speak. She listened as Harry laid out the strange circumstances of the hidden room, and Oliver's suggestion that Polly and the maid involved in the deception of the builders renovating the house might be one and the same person. At last she shook her head, her expression stony. 'I knew she was in with a bad lot, but I never thought she'd turn up dead.' Her gaze met Harry's. 'How did it happen? Was it murder?'

'I don't know. A broken neck could be caused by an accident or a fall, I suppose.' A vision of Polly's waxen face flashed across Harry's mind and she shuddered. 'But she didn't get there by accident. She was placed there for Scotland Yard to find.'

'Not Scotland Yard,' Beth corrected. 'For Sherlock Holmes to find, which puts a very different spin on things. It takes a nasty sort of mind to turn death into a game like that.'

'Yes,' Harry said simply. 'I'm afraid it does.'

Beth took a brooding sip of her pint. 'The other thing I don't understand is how they knew so far in advance that there'd be anything worth nicking.' She cast a sideways look at Harry. 'I've come across a burglar or two in my time and they'd never go to this much trouble unless they were sure there was a big prize at the end.'

It was a thought that had occurred to Harry. The theft had happened overnight, but it had been months in the planning. Someone had known about the connection between Lord Delaware and Prince Rupert, and had predicted it would present a lucrative opportunity. They had also discovered the exact date that the opportunity would arrive, and had executed the crime with masterly precision. They were bold and audacious and supremely confident, and it appeared they had no fear of getting caught. Their name – or at least the name they hid behind – was Professor Moriarty. 'I don't think we're dealing with ordinary burglars,' she replied. 'I think it's an organised gang, the one behind the Lord Robertson job last year. Dora Grubb is in prison for that but the jewellery she stole was never recovered. I've always wondered what happened to it.'

Beth's gaze was shrewd. 'You're thinking of our friend Mr Pole.'

'Not necessarily,' Harry said, and sighed. 'There must be a hundred shops like his in the city, and more than a few that don't ask questions about where the valuables they're offered come from.'

The other woman snorted. 'A few? It's the perfect cover to fence stolen goods. But here's the thing – most criminals would stab each other in the back if there was something in it for them. I reckon a smart gang might have one or two places in London they trust to shift what they steal, and no more.'

It made sense, Harry had to acknowledge. 'Which brings me onto something important. Whoever this gang is, they're dangerous. Polly is dead and – well – I'd rather the same thing doesn't happen to you.' She took a breath and met Beth's gaze. 'I don't want you to undertake any more investigating on my behalf, and if you decide you don't want to work for me in a domestic capacity then I'll understand that too.'

Beth shook her head. 'Not blooming likely. I told my mum I'd found a job and she's already spent half my wages on new clothes for my sisters.' She eyed Harry knowingly. 'Besides, you're not going to stop investigating, are you?'

'No,' Harry admitted. 'But it's one thing putting myself in danger. I can't do the same to anyone else.'

'I see,' Beth said, folding her arms. 'So you've told Mr Fortescue to sling his hook as well, have you?'

Harry paused. 'No, but that's different.'

'Because he's an important lawyer and you need his help.'

'Yes,' Harry said, uncomfortably aware that was only part of the reason she hadn't suggested to Oliver that he back away.

'Thing is, you need my help too. I can go places you can't, talk to people who wouldn't give you or a fancy lawyer the time of day.' Beth leaned forward. 'And Polly makes it personal. She wasn't a bad kid and she doesn't deserve to be treated like a piece in a game. If I can do anything to catch the monster who did that, I will.'

It was no less than Harry expected. Even so, she still felt honour-bound to press the point. 'But—'

'But nothing,' Beth insisted. 'You ain't getting rid of me that easily – there's still the matter of your brother's dodgy engagement, for a start. The clock's ticking on that score – this is her last weekend at the Hot Spot, remember?'

Harry ran a weary hand across her face. After the shocking discovery of Polly's body, the problem of Serafina Eccleston had fallen down her list of priorities. She really ought to relay what

Beth had discovered to Seb, so that the family might at least ensure Rufus could not elope with the girl before all the facts were known. The trouble was that she had yet to uncover anything that proved Serafina had nefarious intentions. Her use of an assumed name was questionable, but Harry couldn't help feeling it was perfectly reasonable – probably even sensible – that she preferred to conceal her identity while working in an illegal club. Hadn't Harry done the same when she'd visited the Hot Spot? Beth was absolutely right – they needed more information and they needed it soon. 'I hadn't forgotten,' she said, sighing. 'Although I confess I have no idea what to do about it.'

Beth tapped her nose. 'Leave that to me. I've got an idea.'

'You're not going to take the job at the Hot Spot, are you?' Harry said, frowning.

'No,' Beth replied. 'But Serafina don't need to know that. I'm going to catch her going into the place this evening, see if I can get her to spill the plan.'

Harry raised her eyebrows. 'Surely she won't tell you.'

The other woman grinned. 'Ah, but we're friends now. And I'm a good listener.'

It wasn't without risk, Harry thought, but it was a good deal less dangerous than their visit to Solomon Pole's shop. She dug into her shabby handbag and pulled out a set of keys. 'These are for my apartment. Obviously, you don't start your domestic responsibilities until Monday morning but if you need somewhere to stay tonight, you're welcome to use the settee again.'

Beth took the keys. 'That's very generous of you. It shouldn't be a late night, but I'll keep it in mind.' She fixed Harry with a determined stare. 'So, what's the plan with Pole? You going to tell Scotland Yard what we suspect?'

It was the sensible course of action, Harry knew, and she

thought Oliver would probably agree. But Sherlock Holmes did nothing without data and she was well aware that she had no evidence to present, nothing but the suggestion that Solomon Pole was more than he seemed. She needed something tangible before she went back to Inspector Wells, and there was only one logical place to look. Turning to Beth, she smiled. 'How do you feel about a visit to the circus?'

* * *

After returning to the poster to check the time of the matinee show, Beth suggested they call into the dressmaker she had visited before their visit to the Hot Spot. 'Just in case the bruiser from the pawnbroker's shop has a good memory. A different hat might confuse him.'

Recalling the glitter of intelligence behind his eyes, Harry agreed, and took the added precaution of purchasing a new coat for each of them to wear. The quality was excellent and the prices so much lower than those at Selfridges that Harry considered them to be a bargain. 'If it's not too much trouble, we'll collect our old coats on the way back from the circus,' she told the dressmaker, as Beth admired her reflection in the mirror.

'As you wish,' the dressmaker said, hanging Harry's drab brown coat on a hanger as though it was made of the finest silk.

'I feel fancy,' Beth said as they made their way back to Liverpool Street to catch the train to London Fields. 'Is this an ostrich feather, do you think?'

'Donated by a grouse,' Harry replied, recognising the cream and brown stripes. 'It suits you.'

'My mum won't know me when I go home,' Beth grinned. 'She'll put my rent up.'

The journey to London Fields was short and uneventful. Hackney wasn't an area of London Harry knew but she was not surprised to see it was heavily industrialised. Factories dominated the skyline to the east, belching smoke from vast chimneys, turning the grey day even more leaden. Beneath the clouds, dilapidated houses and shops skulked along the edges of litter-strewn roads, as though huddling together for protection. Harry did not need to ask for directions to the circus; the train had been filled with well-dressed passengers and children, many of whom had alighted at London Fields station and were clearly bound for the same place. She and Beth followed the crowds as they turned the corner, and saw for themselves the iron railings of the park gates and the vast green space beyond. In the distance, flags fluttered cheerily from the top of an enormous red and yellow tent, while several smaller, less colourful tents sat nearby. At the park entrance, a young woman on a unicycle was jiggling back and forth, balancing in one spot as she waved the crowds onwards. Just beyond her, a juggler tossed an astonishing number of apples and oranges into the sky, grinning at the gasps of the appreciative audience as he caught the fruit and sent it flying again. 'See sword juggling and many more marvels at Cuthbert's Travelling Circus,' he cried. 'But don't delay, today's our last day!'

As they drew nearer to the tents, Harry became aware of an array of enticing smells. Her stomach rumbled, reminding her she had not eaten since breakfast. She glanced at Beth, who was also sniffing the air; they were there to gather information but perhaps it would help them to blend in if they sampled some of the tempting treats on offer. The crowd swelled as they approached the ticket booths at the entrance and it took some minutes for them to purchase two tickets and make their way inside. Immediately, they were approached by a smiling woman in Victorian dress offering to sell them a balloon. Harry waved her away and she moved on. Behind her, a trio of acrobats were tumbling for a small crowd. Recalling Beth's observation from her previous visit, Harry paused to study them but none of them looked small enough to navigate the tunnel beneath Berkeley Square. For all their skill, they could not hold her attention for long. Everywhere she looked, there was something remarkable to see: a majestic elephant being led towards the largest tent, bedecked in paste jewels and tasselled ribbons, an impossibly long-legged stilt-walker who graciously raised his top hat at those passing by, a pair of glossy-coated, gilt-decorated horses being ridden by a young woman with one foot on each of their backs. A splendidly attired black-moustached ringmaster strode around, whip in one hand and a marching cane in the other as he exhorted people to roll up to the greatest travelling show they would ever see. And dotted in amongst all of these wonders were the food stalls, each seller calling out their wares. 'Jellied eels! Fresh from Southend this morning, get your jellied eels here!'

'Meat pies, warm from the oven! Sausage rolls!'

There was no shortage of customers – each stall had a cluster of hungry patrons, keen to buy their wares. Beth tugged on her sleeve. 'Look at that! It's so pretty.'

Harry followed her gaze and saw she was staring at a machine that was spinning sugar into candyfloss. The sugar glistened as the seller wound it expertly around a stick and presented it to a waiting child. 'Would you like some?' Harry asked.

Beth shook her head. 'Nah.'

'Are you sure?' Harry joined the edge of the crowd. 'I'm having a stick.'

A flicker of indecision crossed Beth's face before she gave in. 'Go on, then.'

Harry had not noticed any undue scrutiny as they mingled with the crowd – most people seemed to be too busy taking in the spectacle around them – but she felt better camouflaged behind the swirl of candyfloss. Checking the time, she saw they still had quarter of an hour before the matinee was due to begin. 'Let's try to sneak behind the main tent,' she murmured to Beth. 'We might learn more backstage.'

Affecting casual curiosity, they moved to the edge of the milling crowd. Children's delighted screams rang out as they whirled from the top of the helter-skelter. Harry allowed her gaze to roam past the brightly painted tower to the cluster of dingy cream tents behind the big top. These were not part of the spectacle, plain and unadorned to render them invisible. Nevertheless, she saw they were guarded; a heavy-set, well-muscled man stood with arms folded and legs akimbo as he surveyed the scene. From behind her candyfloss, Harry watched a variety of circus folk pick their way through the maze of ropes that held the tents in place, calling out and pausing to exchange words. There was no sign of the man mountain she had encountered earlier that day, nor did she spy the smaller acrobat Beth had mentioned, but it was clear she had little hope of venturing further without being challenged. Reluctantly, she turned back to Beth. 'Guarded. I wonder why.'

Beth took a large mouthful of candyfloss and chewed. 'Probably to make sure some nosy kid don't get their head bitten off by a lion. It's bad for business when that happens.'

'I can imagine,' Harry said, trying not to picture that particular scene. 'In any case, we should probably take our seats.'

The ring inside the tent was vast, separated from the audience by a circle of low blocks. The ground was lined with sawdust – the pine scent of it tickled Harry's nostrils as they shuffled along the row to an empty space on one of the wooden benches arranged like a giant horseshoe behind the barrier. Overhead, two empty trapezes had been tethered to the sturdy tent poles. At the back of the ring, a pair of golden curtains tumbled from on high, hiding what Harry assumed must be the grand entrance for the performers and animals. The air crackled with expectation as the benches filled with men, women and children. Silence fell. Every face turned to the golden curtains. An unseen band struck up a vibrant, rousing cascade of notes that Harry recognised immediately as 'Entry of the Gladiators'. Trumpets blared, drums thudded and the curtains were drawn back to reveal the portly, red-coated ringmaster. He marched into the ring, beaming and waving his cane in perfect time to the beat, the band following. Behind them there was a stream of dazzling colour: jugglers led acrobats, clowns capered ahead of lion tamers, four glossy horses walked placidly beneath their riders and bird-of-paradise trapeze artists turned somersaults in front of large-muscled strongmen. Automatically, Harry's gaze flew to their bare forearms. None bore the same tattoos as the man they had encountered in Solomon Pole's shop.

'The kid ain't there either,' Beth murmured as the acrobats passed in front of them.

'We will have to be patient,' Harry whispered, with a reassurance she wasn't sure she felt. She could be about to waste an afternoon when time was of the essence.

After looping around the full length of the circle several times, the band led the performers back through the curtains. They dropped shut with a dramatic swish and the music fell away, leaving the ringmaster to take centre stage. 'Ladies and gentlemen, boys and girls, welcome to Cuthbert's Travelling

Circus!' he cried. 'This afternoon, you will witness marvels and miracles beyond your wildest dreams. You will gasp, scream and laugh until you cry. You will be amazed by feats of strength, astonished by acrobatic skills and astounded by the bravery of our fearless animal tamers. Everything you see is real – every danger is deadly. Ladies and gentlemen, boys and girls, prepare to be entertained!'

And they were. One act flowed quickly into another, no more than five minutes long so that the audience did not have time to get bored or even catch its breath. Almost as one, they gasped as the Human Cannonball shot through the air, giggled at the antics of the clowns and covered their eyes when the trapeze artist missed the rung of her swing and caught the outstretched hand of her colleague instead. It was almost thrilling enough to divert Harry from her true purpose, until the acrobats tumbled into the ring. There were eight in total – four men, two women, a girl in her mid-teens and a small boy of perhaps around eleven or twelve, all leaping and somersaulting with dizzying speed. A sharp nudge from Beth told Harry this was the young acrobat she had seen on her previous visit and Harry paid close attention as he twisted and turned. He was certainly slender enough to use the tunnel beneath the house, but it was hard to imagine the exuberance with which he performed turned to darker pursuits. Was it possible he was as nimble with locks as he was in the ring? She could not help hoping her suspicions were wrong.

After a dazzling display that culminated in a precarious human pyramid, the acrobats departed to rapturous applause, which only died down when a gigantic glass tank filled with water was wheeled into the centre of the ring. An excited muttering broke out as five brawny men strained to manoeuvre it into position, hauling on ropes and pushing as the water sloshed around inside. Harry studied each of them. They wore brown coats and flat caps, in the manner of factory workers, which made it impossible to tell whether any of them might be the man they had encountered at the pawnbroker's shop. A shrug from Beth told Harry she had drawn the same conclusion. And now the ringmaster was back, demanding their attention once more. 'She may be small but she is mighty!' he cried, and gestured to the tank. 'Watch, if you dare, as Angelique defies death and escapes the tyranny of not one lock, not five locks but ten steel padlocks as she attempts to save herself from drowning before your very eyes!'

As he finished his dramatic exclamation, the curtain drew back and a slender young woman with hair the colour of flaming coals rode into the ring, standing on the back of a stocky pony. She leapt off while the animal was still moving, landing lightly at the feet of the ringmaster, and Harry was startled to see she barely came up to his shoulder. The crowd cheered as she spun before them, her perfectly made-up face split into a triumphant grin. She threw off the satin dressing gown she wore, exposing a bathing costume that appeared to reveal more than it covered. The man in front of Harry leaned forwards. With great ceremony, the ringmaster reached beneath the tank and withdrew a heavy hessian sack and several lengths of iron chains. Urgent music began to play as the ringmaster wrapped the chains around Angelique and made an enormous spectacle of securing them with padlocks.

'This wasn't part of the show last year,' Beth whispered. 'Lord, I hope she don't drown.'

Harry frowned as she watched. The famous escapologist, Harry Houdini, had performed similar incredible feats throughout his remarkable career and she had no doubt Angelique would have a skeleton key secreted somewhere on her person that would fit all of the locks she was now burdened with. The skill must be in how long she could hold her breath. Even so, Harry felt her pulse quickening as Angelique made ponderous work of climbing the set of stairs beside the tank. She posed for a moment at the top, as though struck by sudden doubt. The ringmaster slammed his cane into the ground, causing several members of the audience to jump. With a tiny, seemingly regretful shake of her head, Angelique recovered her poise and stepped into the tank. The chains sent her plummeting to the bottom. Immediately, she began to writhe. A black curtain was raised, hiding the tank from view, although the very top could be seen – presumably to reassure the audience that no one else had entered it to help. Water sloshed over the top, puffing small clouds of sawdust into the air where it landed. The band continued to play as the ringmaster produced a pocket watch from his waistcoat and made a great show of checking it. 'Three minutes, ladies and gentlemen, and not a second more!'

As exhibitions went, there was not much to see and yet the spectators were on the edge of their seats. As the minutes ticked by, the ringmaster grew visibly agitated, exchanging concerned looks with the men in brown coats and even going so far as to gesture wildly at them to enter the tank. Finally, he threw his arms up in an extravagant sweep. The band reached a crescendo and stopped. At the exact same time, the black curtain cascaded to the floor. As one, every member of the audience sat forward. Angelique floated motionless in the water, her scarlet hair fanned around her head like a terrible, blood-red halo. The chains that had bound her lay discarded beneath at the base of the tank. Seconds passed. She did not move. The woman beside Harry squeaked and covered her face. And then, with a powerful kick that sent more water spilling over the glass sides, Angelique shot towards the surface. Her hands broke free of the water. The crowd erupted into thunderous applause as she hauled herself out, standing at the top of the stairs and dripping, an exultant look on her face as she raised her slender arms aloft.

'The astonishing Angelique!' the ringmaster bellowed, as the diminutive young woman descended the steps to join him in the ring. 'There is not a lock in the world she cannot break!'

Harry watched Angelique bow to each side of the ring, then skip lightly after the tank as it was wheeled from sight, seemingly none the worse for her brush with death. She leaned towards Beth. 'She certainly made short work of those padlocks. I wonder if she'd be equally accomplished with the lock on a safe.'

Beth's eyes narrowed. 'He did say there wasn't a lock she couldn't break. And I reckon she's smaller than my youngest sister. She'd have no trouble with a narrow tunnel.'

It was exactly the thought in Harry's mind too but there was no time to explore it further – the ringmaster was demanding their attention once more. 'And now, prepare to witness the impossible. I present to you the strongest man on earth – Hercules Jones!'

The giant who strode into the ring now wore a deep red leotard bisected by a wide belt, sturdy leather boots and very little else. But Harry barely noticed his costume, nor the heavy weights and dumbbells being placed around him. Her gaze was fixed upon the tattoos that covered his forearms, marking him out as the bruiser she and Beth had met at the pawnbroker's shop. She knew without asking that Beth had observed them too. The ringmaster continued to extol the virtues of his strongman – insisting he could lift weights that would dumbfound them. And Hercules certainly appeared to live up to his mythical namesake, straining muscle and sinew to lift ever-increasing burdens, much to the appreciation of the audience. At last, the ringmaster raised his cane for silence. 'And now for the final feat. Who among our esteemed onlookers would like to claim that Hercules Jones lifted you?'

Tumultuous chatter broke out and several hands shot into the air. Hercules Jones prowled around the edge of the ring, his piggy eyes assessing the volunteers with cold calculation; Harry dipped her head to stare at her neatly folded hands, and she saw the brim of Beth's hat tilt downwards, but it seemed to her that his pace slowed as he reached the bench where they sat. The woman on their right jiggled, clearly desperate to be chosen. Harry did not move.

'Pick me!' her neighbour shrieked. 'Oh, Hercules, pick me!'

Darting the briefest of glances from beneath her hat, Harry felt her heart stutter. The strongman was staring at her, his dense brows knotted together. Instantly, she dropped her gaze once more, scarcely daring to breathe. It was perfectly possible he had spotted her among the sea of faces, had seen past the new hat and coat to recognise her as Miss Peterman, which made her wonder what his next move would be. Would he pluck her from the crowd on the pretext of using her in his act? How should she respond if he did? But a swell in noise and agitation from those seated nearby, and a huff of disappointment from her neighbour, suggested Hercules had moved on. Harry risked another peek and saw, with much relief, that she was correct. After a moment or two more, the strongman made his choice – a middle-aged man with the heavy jowls and protruding stomach of a man who enjoyed his food – and instructed him to sit on a chair in the centre of the ring.

'What is your name, sir?' the ringmaster demanded.

'Albert Dearly,' he replied.

The ringmaster nodded. 'Are you in good health, Mr Dearly? You are not afflicted by maladies of the heart, I trust?'

Albert Dearly looked mildly affronted. 'Not at all.'

'And how much do you weigh, sir?'

At this, Mr Dearly looked a little uncomfortable. 'I don't know that I—'

The ringmaster threw up his hands. 'How are we to marvel at the brilliance of Hercules if we don't know how much weight he lifts? Come now, you may whisper it to me if you prefer.'

Mr Dearly did so. 'Sixteen stones and three pounds!' the ringmaster roared, turning back to the crowd. 'But that is nothing to Hercules. Watch as he balances this sizeable gentleman – chair and all – upon his head!'

Harry's thudding heart began to settle as four brown-coated circus hands came forward and strapped Albert Dearly to the chair with leather belts across his chest and legs. 'For your own safety, sir!' the ringmaster cried, when the volunteer looked as though he might protest.

Once he was secured, the men each gripped a corner of the chair. Squatting so low he almost brushed the ground, Hercules waited as they heaved the chair upwards. Mr Dearly let out an undignified squawk and grabbed the seat. Another assistant placed a plush satin cushion on the top of the strongman's head, then the chair was lowered into position. Muscles bulged as Hercules gripped the legs of the chair. His face reddened. With a grunt of effort that became a full-throated roar, he pushed upwards on legs that suddenly resembled the trunks of mighty oaks. The chair lurched. Mr Dearly covered his eyes. But he did not fall. Steadily, Hercules rose, and the chair moved above him, until at last he stood upright. His face was almost purple, his eyes the size of hard-boiled eggs. Thickened veins protruded from his neck and chest. He let go of the chair legs, allowed a huffing Mr Dearly to balance there for several long seconds, then let out another roar and thrust the man and his chair into the air, straightening his arms so that the burden hovered over his head. Clearly overcome, Mr Dearly screamed. Applause exploded from the crowd, and several people leapt to their feet to cheer, but Harry barely heard. She was no longer in the circus tent. Instead, she found herself transported back to the secret room of 50 Berkeley Square, where the body of Polly Spender had been secured to the chair in much the same way as Albert Dearly. Her gaze travelled upwards to the ceiling, smooth and white but lacking in the brilliant freshness of the recently applied plaster that graced the room next door, and she knew in a flash that she had disregarded one of Sherlock Holmes' most frequently repeated maxims – that once the impossible had been eliminated, whatever remained, however improbable, must be the truth. And yet she doubted even Holmes could have guessed how the thieves came and went from the hidden room without understanding their connection to the circus. She ran a shaky hand across her face and the sawdust ring swam back into view, with Hercules Jones at its centre, taking in the applause. Harry sat perfectly still, her brain whirring as she considered the implications of all she had seen. Could it be that she had just found the final piece in the puzzle of the locked room?

12

Harry scarcely took in the remainder of the performance. The moment the final curtain fell, she got to her feet and began to edge towards the aisle, ignoring the grumbling complaints of those still seated on the benches. Beth followed. 'I vote we make for the station sharpish,' she said in an undertone. 'Before Hercules Jones and his cronies come looking for us.'

'Agreed,' Harry said, glancing over her shoulder to make certain he was not making his way towards them already. 'There's no time to lose.'

Dusk had begun to fall, cloaking London Fields in half-shadow, and sleet stung their cheeks as they hurried across the park. It wasn't until they alighted the train at Liverpool Street and mingled among the crowds there that Harry felt the tension in her shoulders lessen. They left the station in search of a telephone kiosk, to allow Harry to enlist Oliver's help. 'Where are you?' he asked, once the call was connected. 'I've been trying to contact you all afternoon.'

She brushed the question aside. 'Never mind that now. Can you persuade Inspector Wells to meet us at Berkeley Square in half an hour? I want to make sure I'm right before I tell her what I suspect.'

'Half an hour?' Oliver said, evidently taken aback. 'I'll do my best but that won't give us time to disguise ourselves. Are you sure you want Wells to know you're not a man?'

Harry thought of the speculative look she had seen on the inspector's face during their last meeting. 'I think she already knows,' she said. 'I'm still dressed as Sarah Smith, but perhaps it might be prudent to ask if we can use the tradesman's entrance, especially since you won't be disguised at all.'

Once Oliver had rung off, Harry turned to Beth. 'It's too risky to collect our old hats and coats from the dressmaker now. We can stop by for them next week.' She eyed her fretfully. 'Do you have everything you need ahead of speaking to Serafina this evening? I can't help wishing I was coming with you.'

'She'd clam up like an oyster if you did,' Beth pointed out. 'But don't worry, I'll be careful.'

Harry gnawed at her lip. 'I expect that's what Polly Spender said too.'

Beth shook her head. 'I'm sharper than Polly and I ain't mixed up with the same kind of criminals she was. I bet I'll be home before midnight, never you fear.'

As Harry watched her make for the bus that would carry her towards Camden, she could only pray Beth's optimism was justified.

* * *

If Inspector Wells was in any way surprised to be confronted by Harry dressed as a woman, she did not show it. 'Good evening, Miss Smith,' she said crisply, when the police officer stationed at the back door showed her and Oliver into the hallway of number 50 Berkeley Square. 'Mr Fortescue here tells me you are an associate of Mr Thompson, and come with fresh information regarding this peculiar matter.'

'I do,' Harry said, relieved the policewoman seemed disposed to play along, at least for now. 'But before I reveal anything, Mr Thompson has instructed me to ask one or two questions, the answers to which may have an impact upon the case.'

'I shall certainly help if I can,' Inspector Wells said, appraising her judiciously. 'What would you like to know?'

'Were you able to interview Mr Evans about his experiences during the renovations?'

'As a matter of fact, we were. It was all much as your associates said – there were some very strange aspects to the job that made it stand out in his mind. The caretaker was an odd fellow but he let them in each morning. The maid was a nervous little thing. He couldn't recall her name but thought it might have been Poppy.'

'Or Polly,' Oliver put in.

The inspector nodded. 'Mr Thompson was right about the body too – Mrs Spender confirmed it was her daughter this afternoon.'

Harry bowed her head. She had already known, of course, but the confirmation still created a well of sadness for a mother robbed of her child.

'Have you managed to locate the caretaker?' Oliver asked.

'Not yet,' Inspector Wells said. 'I'm sure it will come as no surprise to you that he has not returned to his old address.'

'Indeed not, since he must know that's the first place you will look for him,' Oliver said. 'It's safe to assume he took a copy of the keys to the house before he left.'

'That would explain why there was no evidence of a break-in,' the inspector agreed. 'Although I confess I still can't see how the theft was done.'

Harry cleared her throat. 'Perhaps I can help with that. We know the dining room was in use until midnight on the night of the theft, and the safe was found open just before eight o'clock the following day. I think the thieves entered this house while the family and domestic staff slept, used the tunnel to creep into number 48 and break into the safe, then left the same way they came in.'

'But how?' Inspector Wells threw up her hands. 'How did they access the hidden room?'

Harry smiled. 'For that, we need to examine the carpets upstairs.'

The other woman narrowed her gaze. 'The carpets? Whatever for?'

'Mr Evans reported his men complained of mysteriously creaky floorboards. I suspect the reason for that will soon become clear.'

Oliver was also eyeing her with puzzlement. 'Then by all means let's go.'

Despite endeavouring to sound every bit as assured as Holmes when stating her case, Harry felt the sinuous coils of doubt constricting her stomach as they climbed the staircase to the first floor. Could she be mistaken? Was she seeing connections where none existed? Forcing herself to ignore her misgivings, she paused at the top of the stairs and turned to the landing on the left. 'What's behind here?' she asked, pointing to the first door.

'A music room, I believe,' Inspector Wells said.

Harry closed her eyes for a moment, picturing the dining room below, with its ruined false wall. She progressed along the landing to a second door. 'And this?'

'Mr Anderson's study.'

'I think that may be the one,' Harry said and, before she could lose confidence, she pushed the door back.

Much like the study in the house next door, the floor in this room was furnished with an expensive rug. Almost as soon as Harry stepped across the threshold, a floorboard creaked under her feet. She stopped to scan the floor, noting that the rug did not extend under the desk beneath the window, then fired an enquiring look Oliver's way. 'I wonder if you might help me lift this rug?'

Together, they heaved it out of the way to reveal dark wooden floorboards. Dropping to her knees, Harry ran her hands across them, searching for a tell-tale gap. Finally, she found what she was looking for – a slender crack at the end of one board. 'Could you pass me that letter knife, please?' she asked Oliver.

He took it from the desk without comment, watching as she slotted it into the space and levered the wood upwards. It came away easily, lifting to reveal a long, thin cavity. But that was not all. As she pulled the board away, a lengthy strand of fiery red hair caught the light, snagged on the roughened edge of the wood. Harry looked at it for a moment. 'I don't suppose there's an envelope to hand, is there?'

Oliver cast around. 'No, but there's a sheet of paper.'

'That will do.' Teasing the hair free, Harry tucked it into the folded paper, offering it to Inspector Wells. 'You might want to take this. I think you'll find it matches that of one of your soon-to-be suspects.'

Without waiting for a response, Harry ran her hands along the floorboards once more. The next slid out smoothly and soundlessly, and the board beside that did the same, until over a third of the floor had been removed. She bent to examine the edges of the boards that remained, noting a series of shallow grooves that had been carved into the wood. 'Take note of these, Inspector,' she said, pointing at the indentations. 'They are also a clue.'

In silence, Inspector Wells examined the scuff marks, although it was clear from her bemused expression that she did not yet understand what they meant. Once she stepped back, Harry set to with her fingertips once more, this time exploring the cavity beneath the missing boards, and again she found a break. She dug with the letter knife, scarcely daring to breathe as she levered upwards, and was rewarded as the whole section of floor beneath the boards shifted. Thrusting her fingers into the widened crack, she pulled hard and felt the wood come away. For a moment, all she saw below was darkness, then her eyes adjusted and she saw the barest outline of walls and floor. 'Would one of you be good enough to go downstairs and turn the dining-room light on?' she said, glancing over her shoulder.

Inspector Wells vanished from the room and Harry took the opportunity to examine the raised wooden panel, noting the underside had been painted white to blend in with the ceiling. Moments later, the space below Harry was lit up by a pale-yellow glow that spilled through the hole in the wall, and Inspector Wells appeared. Her face craned up at Harry. 'They lowered the safe-cracker from the room above. The grooves you pointed out were made by the rope.'

'Yes,' Harry said. 'Once inside, they navigated the tunnel, stole the diamond and came out the same way. Perhaps Polly fell from up here in the course of the theft, or perhaps she knew more than was good for her and that led to her death, but at some point, her embalmed corpse was lowered back into the room on the chair.'

Oliver frowned. 'It would take tremendous strength to do that.'

'Exactly,' Harry replied. 'The kind of strength one might expect from the self-proclaimed strongest man on earth.' She returned her attention to Inspector Wells. 'If you hurry, you should be able to catch Cuthbert's Travelling Circus before it leaves London Fields. Their strongman performs as Hercules Jones, although I don't imagine that's his actual name. And the hair in that paper is the exact shade worn by Angelique, an escapologist I saw perform this afternoon. She claims there isn't a lock in the world that can resist her.'

Inspector Wells gave her a penetrating stare. 'The circus?'

'The circus,' Harry confirmed. 'If we're really lucky, you may even find the Sora-Sora diamond there, although I'm more inclined to think Solomon Pole the pawnbroker has that.'

There was a brief silence as the inspector processed the flurry of new information. 'Pole's shop has been known to Scotland Yard for some time,' she said, frowning. 'But we've never been able to pin anything on him. What makes you think he's involved with the theft?'

'Hercules Jones was moonlighting for him as an enforcer when I visited the shop,' Harry said. 'I confess I have no hard evidence Pole is involved with the theft but there's definitely a connection between him and the circus. I suspect he may be the mastermind of the operation.'

Oliver became very still. 'You think he's Moriarty?'

The name caused Harry to hesitate, recalling the almost palpable sense of villainy that had emanated from Solomon Pole. He had been greedy and cunning, eager to take advantage of the desperation of his customers and quick to fall back on the threat of physical violence. At first sight, she had imagined him as a Dickensian crook, but he might just as easily have stepped from the pages of an Arthur Conan Doyle adventure. And yet Harry felt a niggle of doubt. Holmes described Moriarty as an elusive puppet master, one who inhabited a world far removed from the dark deeds he orchestrated. He never dirtied his hands by committing the crimes himself. If the criminal who had planned this crime had modelled himself on the fictional character of Moriarty, it seemed unlikely he would have left a trail of breadcrumbs for Scotland Yard to follow. 'I don't know,' she admitted with a sigh. 'But if Pole isn't Moriarty then he may know who is.'

The inspector puffed out her cheeks, her expression suddenly subdued. 'I doubt we'll find the diamond, in any case. It will have been broken up into smaller stones by now.'

'You might be surprised,' Harry said. 'Whoever Moriarty is, he appears to view crime as something of a game. The theft of the diamond was simply have been a move, not his ultimate goal.'

'Perhaps,' Inspector Wells conceded. 'We'll see what this strongman and the escapologist have to say. I'll gather my officers and go there now.'

Harry got to her feet. 'I'll come too.'

'Absolutely not.' Oliver and Inspector Wells spoke at the same time.

'It's too dangerous,' Oliver went on, his brows furrowed. 'Especially since it seems Jones recognised you at the circus. You've done all you can. Leave the rest to the police.'

Inspector Wells nodded, equally implacable. 'This is not a detective novel, Miss Smith. While I am grateful for your help, Scotland Yard is not in the habit of involving civilians in their arrest and interrogation of suspects. I am grateful for your help to this point but you may leave the remainder to my officers and me.'

Seeing Harry's mulish expression, Oliver placed a hand on her arm. 'Moriarty expects you to leave your King exposed but you're too clever for that. Step back now and let Scotland Yard finish the job.'

Harry swallowed a groan of frustration. It made sense, she knew it did, but the impulse to confront Hercules and Angelique and observe their guilt for herself was hard to quell. 'What if I'm wrong?'

'All the more reason to remain in the wings,' he said, and raised an eyebrow. 'Do you think you're wrong?'

She ran through everything she had learned, the leads she had followed and threads she had connected, the grooves from the rope and the red hair that had been caught between the floorboards. Everything pointed in one direction and if she had learned anything from Sherlock Holmes, it was to follow the evidence. She shook her head. 'No.'

'Then leave it to Inspector Wells.' He pulled a wry face. 'I'm sure we shall read about her brilliance in the papers once the case is wrapped up.'

There was wisdom in his counsel, Harry knew. It often happened this way for Holmes, and he was content to let the police capture the criminals, but she couldn't help feeling somewhat disappointed that she would not see for herself whether the missing diamond was where she predicted. On the positive side, she would not have to endure the vulturous gaze of Solomon Pole again, although she would have liked to have watched his expression as she reclaimed the charm bracelet he had all but stolen. 'I wish you good hunting, Inspector Wells.'

The inspector's smile was hard and glittering. 'You may depend upon it, Miss Smith. Once the prey is in my sights, I never miss my mark.'

* * *

Harry was woken from sleep by an insistent hand upon her shoulder, shaking her gently until her eyes flew open. It took her a moment to absorb that someone stood beside her, and several seconds more to realise that the person illuminated in the half-light from the open door was Beth. Sitting up, her heart thudding from being awoken so abruptly, Harry reached for the bedside lamp and peered at the other woman, taking in her apprehensive expression. 'What is it? What's wrong?'

'Come through to the living room,' Beth said, her expression inscrutable. 'I'll brew some tea.'

She left the bedroom, closing the door behind her. Harry lay back against the pillows. The time on her bedside clock showed it was just past midnight. While she had thought it possible that Beth might return to Hamilton Square after her reconnaissance mission at the Hot Spot, she had not anticipated she would feel the need to wake her. Something must have happened.

In the soft light from the single table lamp in the living room, Harry saw Beth wore the same dress she'd worn on her previous visit to the nightclub. The hem was sodden, she observed, and crusted with dirt, suggesting it had started to rain sometime after she and Oliver had said goodnight and gone their separate ways. A pair of grubby, water-stained satin shoes sat beside the still glowing hearth. Harry frowned. 'Did you walk all the way from Soho?'

Beth looked up from the kettle. 'No. But it took me a while to find a cab I liked the look of.' She sniffed. 'He still tried to charge me an arm and a leg. I think he was a bit surprised when I told him where to get off.'

Harry couldn't prevent a smile as she settled on the settee. 'Good for you.'

'And don't worry about the shoes,' Beth said. 'I know a trick that'll bring them up as good as new.'

'Your shoes are the least of my concerns,' Harry replied, taking in her set expression and the stiffness in her shoulders. 'It's you I'm worried about. Did something untoward happen tonight?'

Beth lifted the tea tray and brought it to where Harry waited. 'You could say that,' she said, grimacing as she reached down to massage her stockinged feet. 'I went to the club, like we planned, only it turned out Serafina weren't working. She'd called in with a headache or some such, according to the lads around the back. Bang went my excuse for being there, but I thought I might be able to do some digging all the same, if I could get inside.'

'How did you manage that?' Harry asked curiously.

'I got a bit lucky there,' Beth admitted. 'I couldn't sweet talk my way in through the staff entrance so I went round to the front, to try my hand with the old girl who keeps the door. And who should I meet on Gerrard Street but your friend Mr Finchem.'

It was the last name Harry had expected to hear. 'Percy?'

'The very same,' Beth confirmed. 'He remembered my name, asked about my plans for the evening and invited me to join his party.'

Harry blinked. 'That was lucky. How did he get you past Nell?'

She shrugged. 'Gave a false name, same as your brother. Millicent Hendry, as I recall. I had a squint at the book when I signed – seems he had quite the party planned. The table was the biggest there – Albert nearly scraped his nose on the floor he bowed so low. Except he wasn't called Albert this time – his name was Jacques, if you please.'

That wasn't a surprise – Harry imagined he adopted a different name every night of the week. It was a code, to protect the premises from unwanted visitors. She narrowed her eyes. 'Was Seb there?'

'I didn't see him if he was. But Percy didn't leave me alone long enough to do much nosing around. He introduced me to all his friends, wouldn't hear of me paying for any drinks and kept topping up my glass.' She sighed with evident regret. 'I had to tip a lot of champagne on the floor when he weren't looking.'

Harry tried not to wince, despite being impressed by her guile. 'It sounds as though he was very attentive.'

'Oh, he was quite the charmer,' Beth said, raising her eyebrows. 'I can see why you like him. But it turns out he only wanted me for one thing.'

Instantly, Harry's heart plummeted. 'Oh, no,' she murmured, her hand covering Beth's. 'He didn't—'

'Not that thing,' Beth said, throwing her an amused glance. 'Trust me, I know how to dampen a man's ardour when he gets a bit fresh, and gentlemen are just as tender as dockers.'

'Oh.' Harry sat back, unsure whether it was Beth's confidence in her ability to defend herself or the fact that she hadn't needed to that reassured her the most. 'Good.'

After a swift swirl of the pot, Beth set about pouring the tea. 'What he really wanted was information about you. At first it was just general stuff, asking after your family, that kind of thing. He said he'd been to Abinger Hall and beaten your brother at cards.'

'He has,' Harry said, recalling that both Seb and Lawrence

had good-naturedly complained about coming off worse in a late-night poker game. 'What else did he ask about?'

Beth gave her a sidelong look. 'He seemed very interested in Mr Fortescue, asked how often you saw each other and wanted to know if I thought you were sweet on him.'

A blush swarmed across Harry's cheeks. She took refuge in a sip of scalding tea and instantly regretted it. 'What did you say?'

'I said I hadn't the faintest idea. And then he asked if you'd found a way to scare off Serafina yet.'

'Serafina?' Harry repeated, lowering her cup to the saucer with a clatter. 'How could he know about that?'

But even as she said it, the pieces fell into place. Percy and Rufus were part of the same social set, and both appeared to be regulars at the Hot Spot. Percy had probably known about her brother's dalliance with the dance hostess long before his family had.

'He didn't say,' Beth replied. 'But he seemed to know all the ins and outs, including the plan to run away to Gretna Green.'

Harry groaned. If Percy knew everything then it seemed likely other clients of the Hot Spot did too, and there had been any number of ferocious gossipmongers present on the night she'd visited. They would have no compunction in spreading the news of a scandalous elopement the moment it happened. She had to find a way to persuade Rufus that his plan could only lead to disaster.

'And then he said he might be able to help,' Beth went on, watching Harry over the rim of her cup. 'If you wanted him to.'

'What?' Harry stared at her. 'How?'

Beth shrugged. 'He said she's got a secret, and that he'd be happy to share it with you. But only you. And only if you meet him in person.' She paused to fix Harry with a meaningful look. 'Tonight.'

'Tonight?' Harry echoed, with a dismayed look at the clock on the mantelpiece. 'But it's very nearly one in the morning. What could be so urgent that it can't wait until a more respectable hour?'

Beth's smile was humourless. 'I think that might be the point. I've got no idea whether this secret he claims to know is going to be useful or not. But he wants you to come alone. No Mr Fortescue or me. Just you.'

'Why?' Harry asked. 'If he really wants to help, why can't he tell Seb, or Lawrence, for that matter?'

'Because I don't imagine he's romantically interested in either of them,' Beth said patiently. She rose and took something from her bag. 'Perhaps this will explain. He asked me to give it to you.'

The letter was written on plain, inexpensive notepaper, but the handwriting was swift and assured.

My dear Miss White,

I have spent a delightful evening in the company of your friend, Miss Lizzie Devine, who informs me you are still struggling with the matter of your brother's entanglement with a young lady of uncertain prospects. If you are able to meet me at the corner of Mason's Yard at two o'clock this morning, we may be able to uncover vital information regarding Miss Eccleston that will prove most beneficial to your family. Time is of the essence as I believe the couple intend to depart for Scotland in secret on Tuesday morning.

Naturally, I make this offer in the strictest confidence, to you and you alone. It does not extend to the steadfast Mr Fortescue, who I fear would only jeopardise our mission. You may rest assured that both your safety and your reputation will emerge unscathed.

Yours in good faith,

Percy Finchem

Harry read it twice, frowning over the address. Mason's Yard was an old mews not far from the London Library, where Harry frequently went to consult the newspaper archives. The entrance was on Duke Street, a mere stone's throw from Quaglino's, and the alleyway where she and Oliver had found themselves the night before. 'I don't understand. Why does Percy want me to meet him there? Do you think that's where Serafina lives?'

'In Mayfair?' Beth snorted. 'Not on the money she takes home from the Hot Spot. But I daresay there may be other nightclubs nearby. Maybe he's expecting to run into her in one of them.'

It was possible, Harry supposed. Mason's Yard was a quiet backwater compared to the more fashionable streets that surrounded it, but the Hot Spot hid behind an ordinary front door in Soho. Wasn't it likely that other illegal clubs did the same? She covered her mouth as a sudden yawn overcame her. 'I'm too tired for this. I wish he'd just tell me what he knows, instead of hinting at it.'

'Perhaps it's something you need to see, rather than hear about,' Beth said. 'Or maybe it's an excuse to get you alone. It might even be both. Are you going to go?'

Harry sighed. 'I'm not sure I have any choice. Serafina herself doesn't think she'll need her job any more and if what Percy says is true, then she and Rufus will be married by the middle of next week. I need to uncover the truth before that happens.'

Beth stirred her tea in silence for a moment. 'How much do you trust Percy?'

It was a valid question, Harry thought. Percy had never been anything other than charming towards her, and he came from an impeccable family. Despite the cryptic warning whispered to her by Louisa that night at the Hot Spot, Harry had no evidence to suggest she should distrust Percy, or the information he claimed they might uncover. Whether she could trust herself was another matter. 'Oliver has a poor opinion of him.'

'I imagine he does,' Beth said, with a smirk that caused Harry to wonder what exactly she thought their relationship was. 'But you're right – you don't really have a choice. Not unless you plan to keep Rufus locked up for the rest of his life.'

That clinched it for Harry. For as much as her little brother could be careless, self-centred and entitled, he was also clever, determined and resourceful. If he had set his heart on marrying Serafina, he would find a way to do it. The only way to be certain whether the marriage would be a mistake was by finding out everything it was possible to know about her, and it seemed help on that score had arrived in the unlikely form of Percy Finchem.

Swallowing a sigh, she put down her cup. 'Come on, then,' she said to Beth, hoping the fatigue in her bones would pass with the application of eau de parfum. 'You can help me find something to wear.'

13

Hamilton Square was deserted when Harry slipped past the door of her apartment block and made for Piccadilly. She did not linger to admire the windows of Fortnum and Mason – a freezing fog had descended that did not encourage dawdling – but hurried on, head down, across Jermyn Street towards Mason's Yard. As she neared the entrance, she made out the fuzzy silhouette of a lone figure sheltering in the lee of the building. 'Percy?' she called in a low voice. 'Is that you?'

The glow of a lit cigarette flared in the moist air as the figure stepped out and she was relieved to see it was indeed Percy Finchem. 'Miss White,' he said, flashing her a welcoming smile that the greyness did nothing to dim. 'How splendid of you to come. Isn't it a perfect night for a clandestine encounter?'

Harry glanced up at the moonless sky, the stars shrouded by a blanket of featureless cloud. She shivered as the chill pervaded her coat. 'It's a little cold for my liking,' she said. 'I hope we don't have far to go.'

'Not far at all,' Percy said, and extended his arm for her to take. 'Shall we?'

She allowed him to guide her through the narrow street that led into Mason's Yard. The fog seemed thicker here, obscuring her vision with veil after veil of wispy grey chiffon. Directly ahead, she could make out the glimmer of a street-lamp, the light diffused by the damp to create a shimmering golden halo. Percy steered her to the left, where doors and shopfronts loomed amid the murk. They passed several, shuttered and black, and then Percy stopped beside an iron railing that guarded a narrow set of stairs leading below street level. Swinging open the gate on hinges that were clearly kept well oiled, he unhooked Harry's hand from the crook of his arm. 'The steps are usually salted but wet weather can make them slippery. Please take care to hold onto the rail as you descend.'

Harry stared past the shadows to a dim light that glowed a short distance below. 'This is where we will find Miss Eccleston?'

'That is the entrance, yes.' His smile was cool, almost amused. 'Were you expecting the doorman from the Ritz?'

She met his gaze squarely, refusing to be cowed. 'No, but nor was I expecting a basement. What kind of establishment is this?'

'I suppose you might call it a members' club,' he said. 'Not specifically for gentlemen, although there are certainly more men than women. Forty years ago, it would have been known as a Hell.'

Harry fought to maintain an unruffled countenance. She had read about such places in the work of Charles Dickens and George Eliot – gambling dens where entire fortunes could be lost in a single game of cards. Some, like the infamous White's or Crockford's on St James Street, had been established in

Regency times for the exclusive use of those with wealth and status, but many more had been aimed at parting the poor and working classes from what little they had. Tireless work by anti-gambling campaigners, including Harry's own grandfather, had improved matters; unlicensed Hells were raided and closed down but, as with illegal nightclubs, that simply meant they moved underground. 'I see.'

Percy laughed. 'Do I sense disapproval, Miss White?'

'Not at all,' she replied, trying not to consider what Oliver would say if he knew what she was about to do. It did not surprise her that Percy was evidently familiar with such establishments. 'Is Miss Eccleston a gambler?'

'I don't believe so,' Percy said. 'Her reason for coming here is more... intimate.'

She stared at him, aghast. Sensationalised reports in the newspapers often claimed that unlicensed gambling went hand in hand with darker criminal activity but surely Percy wasn't suggesting what he seemed to be? 'Have you brought me to a brothel, Mr Finchem?'

Now it was Percy's turn to look shocked. 'Absolutely not. I hope you know I would never expose you to such an environment. Apart from anything else, Fortescue would probably challenge me to a duel, or something equally noble and archaic.'

It was intended to make her smile and it did go some way to soothing her alarm. 'He still might.'

'An excellent point,' Percy said gravely. 'But if you want to understand what is driving Miss Eccleston's affair with Rufus then there is no other way. We shall have to go inside.'

She squared her shoulders. 'Lead on.'

The stone stairs were narrow and steep. Salt crunched under Harry's feet as she followed Percy down into a square well at the bottom. The light that hung there revealed a black front door with a small glass aperture three quarters of the way up. A brass button was set into the wall. There was nothing else, no plaque bearing a name or number, nothing at all to identify it. Harry experienced a curious sense of déjà vu as Percy pressed the button; it appeared that Hells, like illegal nightclubs, set great store by being almost impossible to find if one did not know where to look. After a moment, she heard the sound of a panel being slid back and sensed an eye had been applied to the spyhole. A long silence followed, then she heard the rasp of bolts. The door opened to reveal a gaunt, unsmiling man who did not speak but held out a hand, palm upwards in demand. Percy placed something upon it and Harry was surprised to see it was a long black feather, glossy even in the half-light. Evidently satisfied, the man wrapped his fingers around it and gestured them hurriedly inside.

'After you, Miss White,' Percy said, waving an arm as though inviting her to cross the threshold of a lavish ball.

Hoping she was not about to make a terrible mistake, Harry snatched a final lungful of moisture-laden air and stepped through the door.

The hallway beyond the entrance was barely better lit than the steps had been. It held nothing but an old wooden chair and ended in another door, this one reinforced with dull sheets of iron. The doorman shuffled forwards to rap upon the metal. It was opened by another mute man, who raised an old-fashioned miner's lamp to examine them closely before stepping back. Once again, Percy waved Harry through and, by the glow of the lantern, she saw they were in a roughly hewn passageway paved with uneven flagstones. The door clanged shut and their guide set off, lamp held high to send beams of yellow slicing through the absolute blackness.

'Watch your step,' Percy murmured from behind her. 'The floor can be somewhat treacherous and the slope does not help.'

They walked in this fashion for several minutes, burrowing deeper underground. Once or twice, they were obliged to step across puddles and Harry could hear the drip of water as it hit the flagstones. Occasionally, they turned left or right and she caught glimpses of adjoining passageways that led in different directions. She did her best to create a mental map in her mind but had to accept she was soon hopelessly disoriented. It was a labyrinth, she thought dazedly as she focused on keeping her footing and staying dry, a maze below Mayfair that most people were entirely unaware existed. She and Oliver must have used part of it when they had fled from Quaglino's but she'd had no idea at the time that it might be part of a warren. Where exactly was this gambling den?

It was difficult to judge precisely how long they walked for – Harry guessed it to be a little under fifteen minutes, but she could not say how far they had travelled. It was entirely possible that their wordless guide had led them a circuitous route to ensure their final destination remained untraceable, but at last their journey ended at another iron-plated door.

The brightness of the room beyond it momentarily blinded Harry. She blinked hard, waiting for her vision to adjust, and realised she could hear music. Percy's hand rested on the small of her back, gently encouraging her to move forward, and she saw they were in a richly furnished room that put her very much in mind of a plush gentleman's club. Bright fleur-de-lys wallpaper adorned the walls, a rich ruby carpet covered the floor and a brilliant chandelier hung from the ceiling. Several doors led off into more softly lit rooms where Harry glimpsed figures gathered around tables or lounging in chairs. Cigar smoke laced the air, creating a lazy fug that made it hard to discern much detail but somehow added to the aura of decadence and unspoken wealth. All in all, it was a stark contrast to the dank, murky passages she had just negotiated.

A middle-aged man in a well-cut dinner suit hurried forward to greet them. His russet moustache quivered as he nodded at Percy. 'Mr Finchem, how wonderful to see you, and I am delighted to observe you have brought a most charming guest. Won't you introduce us?'

'This is Miss Doone,' Percy said smoothly. 'A close friend of mine.'

The man smiled in a manner that did not quite reach his eyes, and Harry got the impression that she was being assessed in much the same way a farmer might consider a prize cow presented for inspection. 'Any friend of Mr Finchem is most certainly a friend of mine,' he said. 'Welcome to the Black Feather Club, Miss Doone.'

Harry inclined her head, understanding now the unusual calling card Percy had presented to the doorman. 'How do you do?'

'Very well indeed, Miss Doone, and I thank you for asking,' he said, his smile widening. 'What's it to be this evening, Mr Finchem? Poker? Brag?'

Percy tapped his chin, as though considering. 'I think poker, to begin with.'

'As you wish. There's an excellent game underway in the Brummell room, and another about to begin in Cavendish.'

Taking Harry's hand, Percy tucked it under his elbow. 'We'll take a look. Thank you, Cartwright.'

The man bowed and backed away. Percy patted Harry's hand. 'What would you like to drink? Champagne?'

'Nothing, thank you,' Harry said, aware of the tight knot of anxiety that was forming in her stomach. 'Please show me what you've brought me here to see.'

'All in good time,' Percy replied. 'You'll stand out if you don't have a drink. We need to blend into the background, stalk our prey without them even realising we are here.'

Harry sighed, loathe to admit he was right but knowing she needed to look as though she belonged there even if she had never felt more out of place. 'Very well. I suppose it will have to be champagne.'

He snapped his fingers and a waiter appeared with a tray of golden flutes, seemingly from nowhere. Percy took two, held one out to Harry and smiled as he raised the other. 'To illicit adventures, Miss White.'

The first room they entered appeared to be home to a very serious game of poker. Five men sat grouped around a table, with a smartly dressed dealer wearing a green shade over his eyes. Cards were demanded and thrown away with little conversation. Drinks went untouched. A long table lined with cooked meats, breads and salad was largely ignored. Smoke rose languidly into the air, pooling around the chandelier and creating swirls of hazy cloud. Percy leaned towards Harry. 'The young man in the grey suit with the extravagant moustache is a bonnet,' he whispered.

Harry's gaze flew to the man he described, who was now grinning broadly at his companions as the dealer used a rake to push a large amount of money his way. 'A bonnet? What's that?'

'An imposter,' he murmured. 'A false player put into the game by the establishment to entice others to gamble more. Sometimes, he wins and makes a great fuss of showing how much fun he is having. On other occasions, he appears to lose large amounts, which attracts those of a more predatory nature.'

Harry turned to stare at him. 'That's terrible.'

Percy shrugged. 'It's business. Anyone stupid enough not to spot a bonnet deserves to lose.'

Scarcely mollified, Harry studied the young man more closely. He was still smiling but she thought she detected a tightness around his eyes, a touch of melancholy in the way he held himself. But he clearly knew how to gamble – how could he do his job otherwise? 'Why do they do it? Surely they don't enjoy playing if they never really win or lose.'

'They owe the establishment money,' Percy said, sipping his champagne. 'In most cases, they've lost everything they own and have no option but to work here to repay the debt.'

That went some way to explaining it. She felt an unexpected wash of pity. 'And I suppose they were previously encouraged to gamble by someone else in the same situation. It never ends.'

He dipped his head. 'The highs and lows of gambling. In some cases, the debt is so large that members of their family are obliged to work alongside them.'

'But that's little better than slavery,' she protested. 'It can't be legal.'

'Perhaps not, but the alternative is utter ruin.' He paused to drain his glass. 'The golden rule when gambling is never to wager anything you can't afford to lose.'

Harry eyed the intense concentration on the faces of the men who were being dealt a fresh hand. From the looks of things, every single one needed to win. She took a deep breath and forced her pity to one side. 'What does this have to do with Miss Eccleston?'

'All in good time,' Percy reassured her. 'If we move too fast we will frighten her off. Why don't we try another room?'

It was the last thing Harry wanted to do but, once again, she realised she had little choice. She had not noticed any windows, which supported her assumption they were still underground, nor was there any sign of a staircase, which meant she was dependent upon Percy to lead her out of the Black Feather Club. Gritting her teeth, she nodded. She could only hope he would be as good as his word.

The game in the next room did not appear to have started. Several men were clustered around a sideboard laden with bottles of sherry and port, helping themselves while the dealer arranged packs of cards on a green-clothed table. There were women in this room; Harry could not tell if they were players or their companions. They eyed her with curiosity – one or two smiled at Percy – but none approached them.

'Can you spot the bonnet in this game?' Percy asked, switching his empty champagne flute for a glass of claret wine.

Harry allowed her gaze to sweep across the occupants of the room. She dismissed a florid-faced, portly gentleman in late middle age almost instantly – his suit was too well made and his gait too unsteady to be a man at work, unless he was an actor of supreme skill. A silver-haired man with impressive whiskers also seemed an unlikely prospect, but the pallid young man he was talking to was considerably more likely. She was about to say as much to Percy when a flicker of movement from the dealer drew her attention. He sat composedly at the table, his gloved hands shuffling a deck of cards, but his eyes were not focused on his task. Instead, they were fixed on a woman in a scarlet dress, with waves of auburn hair and a cigarette in her hand. She was laughing at something the portly man had said but, as Harry watched, her gaze slid momentarily to the dealer and she gave a tiny, almost imperceptible nod.

'It's the woman in red,' Harry told Percy.

He beamed at her. 'Well done. Perhaps we'll make a gambler out of you yet.'

'Oh, I know how to play.' She offered a thin-lipped smile. 'Ask any of my brothers.'

'I don't doubt it,' Percy replied, grinning in evident delight. 'Is there anything at which you don't excel?'

'Patience,' Harry fired back. 'And I don't mean the card game.'

Percy winced. 'Touché. Goodness knows I have no intention of testing your forbearance, Miss White. Let's take our hunt off the beaten track.'

Ignoring the other, as yet unvisited rooms, he led her to a door in the far corner. At the end of the thickly carpeted corridor beyond it, he opened another. The room beyond was not as brash as those they had just left. In fact, it seemed to Harry as though everything, from the lighting to the furnishings, was more muted here. There were doors, some open wide and others ajar, offering glimpses of rooms that seemed to Harry to be much the same as those they had already visited. Music played, although she could not establish from where, and a waiter offered her a fresh glass of champagne. Percy wandered slowly from door to door, pushing them back and glancing through with little apparent interest, yet Harry suspected he was taking an inventory of everything and everyone inside, absorbing every detail and filing it away. She was beginning to appreciate that there was not much that escaped the attention of Percy Finchem. 'Ah,' he breathed as they entered the last room. 'There you are.'

Harry followed the direction of his gaze, expecting to see Serafina. Instead, her eyes were drawn to a young man of around twenty-five. He was lounging in a chair beside the gaming table, one arm draped across the back, his long legs sprawled in front of him. His dark hair was too long, brushing the collar of his white shirt, and his eyes burned with contempt as he surveyed those around him. A glass of red wine sat untouched upon the table and Harry thought she would not have been surprised if he had leapt to his feet and tossed it into the face of the nearest fellow gambler. And yet for all his sullen fury, he was an attractive man, with high cheekbones and generous lips. Several of the women in the room were darting coy glances his way, along with one or two of the men. If he was the bonnet, he was making absolutely no effort to blend in. 'Who is that?' she murmured, scarcely able to drag her gaze away.

'Hugo de Courcy,' Percy replied. 'Rumoured to be the illegitimate son of the Earl of Dover, although he gets his looks from his mother. Unfortunately, he's also a compulsive gambler. I think you can probably work out the rest.'

'But the Dover estate is vast,' Harry replied, her forehead furrowing. 'Legitimate or not, surely his father can cover his debts.'

Percy's eyes glittered. 'He might well have, had it not been for the small matter of an ill-advised elopement.' He lifted an eyebrow. 'With a dance hostess, I seem to recall.'

Harry stared at him. Examples of wealthy men having their heads turned by a pretty face were nothing new, but she could not ignore the coincidence. 'Do you mean—'

'And here is the other half of our quarry,' Percy cut in, turning to watch the entrance of a blonde-haired woman Harry had seen once before, walking down a staircase beside Beth at the Hot Spot. 'The present Mrs de Courcy, I believe.'

At once, everything dropped into place. 'Mama was right,' Harry breathed, as she watched Serafina Eccleston pause to drop a kiss on the head of Hugo de Courcy. 'She does only want Rufus for his money. But if she's already married...'

'I imagine she was hoping to keep that information to herself,' Percy said dryly. 'At least until after she'd milked your brother for the funds to clear Hugo's debts. Once that was achieved, she would probably have left him.'

Indignation burned in Harry's chest at the thought. Rufus could be headstrong and irresponsible, but he was also loveable and generous, and she had no doubt he thought himself in love with Serafina. He did not deserve to be so cruelly used. Drawing herself up to her full height, Harry thrust her glass into Percy's hands.

'What are you going to do?' he asked, looking more amused than alarmed.

She took a fortifying breath. 'I'm going to make sure Serafina Eccleston, or Ida de Courcy, or whatever she calls herself, breaks off her engagement to Rufus and never comes near my family again.'

Percy nodded, as though he had expected nothing else. 'And how are you going to do that?'

At that moment, Serafina looked around the room. Her eyes came to rest upon Harry and she visibly paled. Reaching into her handbag for the money she had tucked there before leaving her apartment, Harry smiled. 'I'm going to beat her husband at poker.'

14

News of the recovered Sora-Sora diamond did not become public until Monday morning, but the story dominated the headlines of every newspaper.

MISSING DIAMOND DISCOVERED!
Criminal Gang Unearthed at Circus
Death in Mayfair an Accident

Beth had bought several copies of the most popular morning editions on her way to Hamilton Square, allowing Harry the luxury of taking in the details over a breakfast of tea and toast and a soft-boiled egg.

'It says they found the diamond in the false bottom of a costume chest belonging to Angelique Monroe,' she said, without looking up. 'Along with several items from other burglaries around the country, including a necklace belonging to Lord Robertson's wife that was stolen last year.'

Beth grunted. 'I'd have shifted them sharpish.'

'Me too,' Harry replied. 'But I don't suppose she expected to get caught.'

'And she wouldn't have, if it wasn't for you,' Beth pointed out. 'Did it all happen how you said?'

Harry scanned the tiny newsprint. 'It appears that way. Hercules Jones admitted his involvement but claimed Polly fell to her death in the process. He says embalming her was Angelique's idea, to prevent the body from being discovered until after they'd got away.'

Beth looked up from checking the teapot, her expression disbelieving. 'Seems like a lot of trouble to me. Risky, too. They'd have been better off chucking her in the Thames.'

It was a thought that had occurred to Harry too. 'I think they were made to do it. By someone who saw an opportunity to use poor Polly to send a twisted message and gave precise instructions about what needed to be done.'

'Moriarty.' Beth spat the name like a curse. 'What about the letter? How do they explain that?'

'There's no mention of it,' Harry said, frowning. 'I'll have to remember to ask Inspector Wells.'

'How about our friend Solomon Pole? Did they catch him too?'

Harry forced down a now familiar quiver of unease at the mention of his name. 'It says Scotland Yard raided the shop in connection with the theft, but it was empty, completely cleaned out.' She paused and checked herself. 'Or almost completely. Pole himself has vanished.'

The other woman was quiet for a moment. 'Do you really think it's him? That he's Moriarty, I mean?'

It was a question that had plagued Harry for most of Sunday afternoon. She'd awoken long after midday, and it had taken her several moments to realise that her visit to the Black

Feather Club had not been a dream. Serafina had tried to warn Hugo who Harry was, but he could not back out of the game, not without losing face in front of the gamblers around him and risking the wrath of his employers by refusing to play. Harry had been relentless, pretending to herself that it was just another poker game with her brothers, played for matchsticks. She did not win every hand, and at one point she came very close to disaster, but a lucky card from the dealer surprised her, especially since she had assumed he would be favouring the bonnet. One by one, the other players folded, leaving just Harry and Hugo at the table. At last, with a cry of rage she thought to be genuine, he threw down his cards and stormed from the room. Serafina tried to follow but Percy blocked her and the moment the dealer pushed Harry's winnings towards her, she was on her feet and heading towards the pale-faced woman. 'I think we need to talk. Don't you?'

She had accepted the payment Harry had offered, as she'd known she would, just as she had agreed to write a letter that would end her relationship with Rufus. 'I don't care what you use this money for, but please don't attempt to fool another unsuspecting young man into marrying you,' Harry said, her tone deceptively pleasant as Serafina scrawled her signature across the bottom of the letter. 'I will be watching, Mrs de Courcy. And so will my friends.'

Upon leaving the Hell, Percy had insisted on escorting her home and Harry had to admit she was glad of his chivalry. It was almost dawn, the birds were chirping from the rooftops, and she had been awake for the best part of twenty-four hours. Her feet ached and her brain felt as though it had been liquefied. She was not entirely sure she remembered where Hamilton Square was.

'Has anyone ever told you how remarkable you are, Miss

White?' Percy said, when they reached the door of her apartment block.

'Once or twice,' Harry admitted, because she was too exhausted to be coy. 'Thank you for your help this evening. I'm not sure I would have discovered the truth about Serafina in time without it.'

He smiled. 'Believe me, I should be thanking you. Watching you beat the house is the most fun I've had in ages. Cartwright will be asking who you are for months.'

She felt a small pang of guilt then, for all the other gamblers who had lost to her. This was why she never played for anything other than matchsticks. 'I hope you don't get into any trouble.'

His laugh sounded genuinely delighted. 'I assure you I will not. They will be begging me to bring you back, in spite of the monstrous hiding you gave them.' He gazed into her eyes, and it belatedly occurred to her that this time, he really might kiss her. But instead, he reached out to touch her cheek. 'Get some sleep. And perhaps, when you've fully recovered, you'll let me take you somewhere more respectable.'

Another wave of guilt assailed her then, because she could picture Oliver's reaction if she were to accept Percy's offer. Oliver, who had no idea she had spent the night gambling with Percy Finchem and was still patiently waiting for her to answer his question about whether the two of them might be more than simple friends and partners in fighting crime. But she could not deny that she had enjoyed Percy's company, if perhaps not the events of the night itself, and part of her thrilled at the idea of getting to know him better. If only it didn't feel like a betrayal of her best friend...

'I don't know,' she said honestly, as she fought off a yawn.

'Right now, I'm too tired to think of anything more adventurous than climbing the stairs.'

'Perfectly understandable,' he said, and stepped backwards to let her escape. 'Sleep well. I hope we'll see each other again soon.'

At least her mother had been satisfied with the way things had turned out, Harry thought as she pushed the memory of Percy away. She'd given Seb the job of delivering the truth about Serafina's intentions, without revealing exactly how she had come by the information, and he had gone to Abinger Hall to drop the hammer blow that same afternoon. Understandably, Rufus had not taken the news well. At first, he had refused to believe it, furiously accusing Seb of taking their mother's side to destroy any hope of future happiness, even when presented with the letter Harry had obtained from Serafina, tersely explaining that she did not love him and could never marry him. It was only when their father telephoned the Duke of Dover and asked him to confirm the sorry circumstances of his son's marital status and poor choices that Rufus had been forced to accept the unhappy truth. 'I daresay he'll get over it,' Seb told Harry over the phone when he called late on Sunday evening. 'Give it a week and he'll have forgotten her name.'

It would take much more than a week, Harry suspected, and felt enraged all over again at the callousness with which Serafina had used her brother. But the anguish would ease, with time and the support of those who truly loved him, and perhaps it might even encourage him to be a little more careful with his heart the next time a pretty girl smiled at him. Perhaps.

A restless movement from Beth roused Harry from her thoughts. 'I don't know about Pole,' she said, dragging her mind with some difficulty back to the question that hung unanswered between them. 'The fact that he was clever enough to evade capture by Scotland Yard makes me think he was one step ahead all the way.' She hesitated, remembering something else Oliver had mentioned when he'd called on Sunday evening. 'And then there's the charm bracelet.'

'The bracelet?' Beth repeated, and scowled. 'I suppose he took it with him, did he?'

Harry shook her head. 'It was the only thing left in the shop. On the counter, Inspector Wells said, as though it was waiting to be found.' She met Beth's surprised gaze. 'It has to mean something, don't you think?'

'Maybe,' the other woman said, her expression doubtful. 'But we gave a false name and address. There's no way it links back to you.'

'No, I know,' Harry agreed, because Oliver had said much the same thing. 'But I can't shake the feeling it's not a coincidence. I don't think we've heard the last of Solomon Pole.'

'He'll be halfway across the country if he's got any sense,' Beth observed with her usual practicality. 'With a bit of luck, the police will pick him up before he can even catch his breath.'

They could only hope, Harry decided. Pushing the remains of her breakfast aside, she got to her feet to dress for work. It wasn't until she was almost ready to leave for Baker Street that Beth let out a gasp and sat bolt upright on the settee, a copy of *The Times* in her hands. 'Did you look at the personal column this morning?'

Harry felt a chill of dread seep into her bones. 'No. Why?'

Beth thrust the newspaper towards her. 'There's a message. From him.'

Willing herself to stay calm, Harry took the paper and scanned the columns until she saw a familiar name.

My charming Sherlock Holmes,

Congratulations on your victory. I look forward to our next game.

Professor James Moriarty

'Our next game,' she said, looking into Beth's eyes and seeing her own apprehension mirrored there. 'This isn't over.'

'No,' Beth agreed, and her expression settled into a grimace. 'I've got a nasty feeling it's only the beginning.'

* * *

MORE FROM HOLLY HEPBURN

ACKNOWLEDGEMENTS

As ever, I owe thanks to so many people for their help and advice in producing *The Locked Room*. This is a non-exhaustive list – profuse apologies to those I have missed. It goes without saying that any mistakes are my own.

Thanks, always, to Jo Williamson of Antony Harwood Ltd, for her unceasing work on my behalf. I am grateful to all at Boldwood Books, but most specifically to my editor Rachel Faulkner-Willcocks, whose excellent suggestions and comments guided me to make this a better book.

A heartfelt thank you to Cecily Blench for her brilliant copy-editing skills, and Rachel Sargeant for her sharp and detailed proof reading. Your hard work is very much appreciated. Further thanks to Hayley Russell, for making the words into a book, and to the Boldwood design team for coming up with another eye-catching cover. Thank you to Wendy Neale, Nia Beynon and Marcela Torres for their marketing and PR support, and the rest of Team Boldwood for their industry.

The Locked Room is dedicated to Francis Green, whom I declare to be a raconteur and *bon vivant* beyond compare. One evening last year, I asked him about Quaglino's, where he was the general manager for many years, and this led to the revelation that he discovered a long-forgotten, dusty stash of vintage wine in the cellars when he first took up the job. The story of what happened next was a gift, as are all his other tales, and I am immensely privileged to be allowed to hear them. Likewise,

I am incredibly lucky to be able to draw on the expertise of Pauline Green, housekeeper at some of London's most prestigious establishments, who advised me on how distinguished guests might manage their jewels when staying in top hotels. Thank you both.

I am grateful to Brian Parsons, of the London Association of Funeral Directors, for graciously humouring my odd questions about the plausibility of covertly embalming a body in the 1930s, and helping me to devise the fate of poor Polly's corpse.

The most excellent Charlotte Dennis cheers on every book I write, including this one – thank you for always being there. And as ever, my thanks and eternal love go to T and E, as well as to Luna the Labrador for being my very best girl.

Last of all, I want to thank my readers old and new, who encourage me to improve with each story I write. I hope you've enjoyed Harry's third adventure.

ABOUT THE AUTHOR

Holly Hepburn writes escapist, swoonsome fiction that sweeps her readers into idyllic locations, from her native Cornwall to the windswept beauty of Orkney. With *The Missing Maid*, her first book published by Boldwood Books, she turns her hand to cosy crime inspired by Sherlock Holmes himself. Holly lives in leafy Hertfordshire with her adorable partner in crime, Luna the Labrador.

Download your exclusive bonus content from Holly Hepburn here:

Follow Holly on social media:

instagram.com/HollyH_Author
threads.com/@hollyh_author

ALSO BY HOLLY HEPBURN

The Baker Street Mysteries

The Missing Maid

The Cursed Writer

The Locked Room

POISON & pens

POISON & PENS IS THE HOME OF
COZY MYSTERIES SO POUR YOURSELF
A CUP OF TEA & GET SLEUTHING!

DISCOVER PAGE-TURNING NOVELS FROM
YOUR FAVOURITE AUTHORS &
MEET NEW FRIENDS

JOIN OUR
FACEBOOK GROUP

BIT.LYPOISONANDPENSFB

SIGN UP TO OUR
NEWSLETTER

BIT.LY/POISONANDPENSNEWS

www.ingramcontent.com/pod-product-compliance
Lightning Source LLC
LaVergne TN
LVHW030920080826
845145LV00013B/2978

* 9 7 8 1 8 3 5 3 3 7 6 3 9 *